THE SYNDICATE

A DI ERICA SWIFT THRILLER
BOOK 14

M K FARRAR

The Syndicate
A DI Erica Swift Thriller
Book Fourteen
Copyright © 2024 M K Farrar

Edited by Emmy Ellis
Cover Design by Marissa Farrar
Published by Warwick House Press

Exclusive offer for Erica Swift readers! Get 25% off your order using the following code at MK Farrar's direct store: NEPHKVYNSX66 Get great deals on eBooks, audiobooks, and signed paperbacks direct from MK Farrar at mkfarrarbooks.com

---

Get a free book when you sign up to M K Farrar's newsletter mkfarrar.com

---

If you're in the UK, you can now order signed paperbacks from MK Farrar! https://www.tiktok.com/@thrillerstokillfor

ONE

A finger, tipped with a sharp, fake nail, jabbed him in the small of his back, rousing him from sleep.

"Darren," Vicki hissed. "Wake up. I think there's someone downstairs."

He let out a groan and huddled down deeper into the duvet. There was no one downstairs. She'd probably had a bad dream and now was being paranoid.

Her finger stabbed into the fleshy part on the side of his spine again. Those nails cost more each month than his mobile phone bill.

He ground his teeth and forced himself to remain calm. "What is it?"

"I heard something," she insisted. "You need to go and check."

They were in a four-bedroom house one street away from the docks of the Isle of Dogs in East London—a house that was far too big for just the two of them really. Their neighbours were all bankers and accountants, or worked in publishing. Very rarely was there any trouble in this area.

He blinked at the LED clock. It was 3.30 a.m. Middle of the bloody night.

"Darren!" she insisted.

With a huff of frustration, he threw back the bedcovers. "Okay, okay. Fine. I'll check." Then he remembered himself. "Anything to make you happy, my love."

He couldn't see her properly in the dark but got a vague impression of the shape she created under the duvet, and the overly bleached-blonde hair spread over her pillow. How could she have heard anything anyway? The property was a townhouse built on three levels, and their bedroom, the master suite, which took up much of the entire floor, was on the top. Even when he was downstairs, and she was in the bedroom, she didn't seem to hear him even when he was standing at the bottom of the stairs and yelling at the top of his lungs that dinner was ready. He'd taken to texting her instead lately to save his voice. But now, at half past three in the morning, she suddenly had the hearing of an owl.

Victoria prided herself in being clever, but she wasn't always. Maybe she was smart when it came to words and numbers—she was the one who'd bought this big house and was responsible for the Range Rover on the drive-away after selling her own marketing company—but she definitely wasn't always *street* smart. That's where he came in, or so he always told himself.

"Be careful," she said from behind him.

He didn't really think he had anything to be careful about. It was just her overactive imagination. She liked to think of him as her protector, at least physically. He was younger and fitter than she was, and he was the one responsible for doing all the practical stuff around the house—changing the light bulbs and mowing the lawn and taking the bins out.

He climbed out of bed, wearing only his boxer shorts. The air was chilly, and he already regretted leaving his warm spot under the duvet. He ran his hand over his stomach, conscious that it was starting to bulge a bit over the top of his waistband. He was forty-six now, and it wasn't as easy to keep trim anymore. He'd need to watch himself. While he didn't think women wanted some muscle-bound man, he also knew they wouldn't be interested in someone who'd let himself run to fat. Though he believed women also didn't want someone thinner than they were.

Not that he had that concern with Victoria. She kept herself too thin, her collarbones protruding almost painfully beneath her skin. He tried to tell her—kindly—that once a woman got beyond a certain age, it wasn't a bad thing to accumulate a few extra pounds, it stopped the skin looking like it was hanging off her bones, too, but, of course, she didn't listen to him. She carried on being afraid to eat carbs, and God forbid she ever treated herself to a pudding.

He let out another sigh, just to make sure she understood that this was a big imposition on him, and then headed to the bedroom door. They slept with it shut, even though there was no one else in the house, because Vicki had read something about how you were safer if there was a house fire, with your bedroom door closed. That's how she was about these kinds of things—paranoid. It was ironic that she wasn't paranoid in other parts of her life. She'd welcomed him into her home, and her bed, quickly enough.

Darren cracked open the door and peered out. He

didn't believe what she'd said about there being someone else in the house, but there was no harm in exerting a bit of caution.

He strained his ears, trying to hear if there was anything in Vicki's fears. Only silence greeted him.

Letting out another frustrated sigh, he made his way across the landing, towards the stairs. He knew just checking from the top of the stairs wasn't going to placate her. He'd need to poke his head into every room and double-check the front and back doors were locked, too.

Had he locked them? He tried to think back to that evening, before they'd come to bed. *Had* he locked the doors? No, Vicki had come to bed after him, so that had been her job. She had been forgetting things more easily lately, though. She said it was her age, but he'd switched off listening when she'd started mentioning the menopause. He shuddered. He didn't need to hear about things like that. It was a woman's business.

Not that it mattered if the doors weren't locked. No one was down there.

He took the first couple of stairs. The third step down creaked under his weight, and he paused, drawing a breath which remained trapped in his lungs. His heart beat faster.

Why the fuck was he getting anxious? He was letting Victoria get to him. There was no intruder to hear him coming.

He kept going, forcing himself to walk normally, even though all the hairs on the backs of his arms stood on end and his pulse tripped too fast. He was starting to wish he'd stopped to put on a t-shirt or even a pair of jogging bottoms. Maybe it would have been better if he'd picked up his phone as well.

But doing any of those things gave Vicki credibility, and he hadn't wanted to do that either. He wanted to wander around downstairs for thirty seconds, check the doors were locked, and then climb the stairs and get back into bed.

Darren reached the first floor, and, deciding that no one was going to be hiding out in either of the bedrooms or the bathroom, he kept going. The ground floor was where he needed to check. He pictured Victoria still lying in their lovely warm bed, the bedcovers pulled up to her chin, waiting for his return. If he got back only to discover she'd gone back to sleep, while he'd been stalking around the house in his boxer shorts for her, he wasn't going to be happy.

His bare feet hit the cool tiles on the floor at the bottom of the stairs. It was cold, even for November. He didn't like leaving the central heating on overnight, but they might start needing to if it got much colder. He wished he'd left a light on down here, but the only light he had was that of the street beyond the glass in the front door.

Movement came from behind him, the subtle sound of soft footsteps.

Darren spun around, a dark shape deepening the shadows.

"What the fu—"

His blood ran cold. The sweat on his brow turned to ice. He needed to do something, yell out to Vicki to call the police, or try and tackle the intruder, but he couldn't. He was pinned in place, his feet in concrete blocks on the floor.

Through the glass in the front door, a car's headlights caught the black cylinder of metal in front of his face.

She was right, he thought in disbelief. *Fucking hell, Vicki was actually right.*

Someone was in his house, and they were holding a gun, aiming it directly at him. The weapon trembled in the person's grip, their fingers encased in a glove. A black balaclava covered their face.

For a moment, he felt as though he was outside of his body, looking in. Was he still dreaming? This kind of thing didn't happen in real life, did it? This was the setting from a film he might have watched on a Saturday night, while nursing a beer in front of the television.

But then he sank back into his body again, everything becoming crystal clear.

"You asked for this," the person said.

Darren turned to run, a deep part of him already knowing it was too late.

He heard the gunshot before he felt the bullet. The crack of it punched through the air, ringing in his ears. A split second later, he experienced that punch in his back, high up, right at the point where his spine became his neck.

It was as though someone had cut all the muscles in his body. His legs turned to spaghetti, and his arms lost all feeling, and he dropped to the cold tiles, though now he barely felt them.

Was the intruder going to go after Vicki next?

Hide, he willed her. *Grab your phone and hide and call nine-nine-nine.*

But instead, he heard her voice from upstairs. "Darren? Oh my God, Darren!"

It was the last thing he ever heard, and a final thought went through his head... *I had it coming.*

TWO

DI Erica Swift tugged her coat tighter around her body and shivered. It was late November, and, at this time in the morning, it felt like midwinter. The cold crept beneath the collar of her coat and slipped up the insides of her sleeves with its icy fingers. She wanted to stuff her hands into her coat pockets, but instead she snapped on a set of gloves, preparing herself to enter the scene of the crime.

The stark metal towers of Canary Wharf lit up in the distance. There was something futuristic about them—like the skyline of something she might see on a sci-fi show. As with much of London, this area was a combination of tall tower blocks, new-build flats, and industry.

"Sorry for the early start, Detective," the officer in charge of the scene said as she approached.

"I'd say I'm used to it," she replied, "but do we ever really get used to it?"

"I'd prefer not to." He cleared his throat and introduced himself. "Sergeant Parsons, by the way."

The police sergeant had a smooth, pale face that caught the surrounding street lights. She'd place him in his mid-thirties, though she was finding it harder and harder these days to figure out a person's age from their appearance alone.

"DI Swift."

The road was lined by three-story, red-brick townhouses, all fairly new builds. Expensive cars, though most of which were probably on finance, were parked in the driveways. The builders had forgone front gardens, aware that parking was far more of a premium in this area than a patch of grass. Though it was edging towards the crazy time of Christmas, the street wasn't lit up by twinkling lights just yet, but, instead, the swirling blue lights of the multiple police response vehicles and a couple of ambulances illuminated the street.

Erica glanced around for her partner. DS Shawn Turner hadn't arrived yet, and his absence stirred mixed feelings inside her. While she wanted him by her side, sometimes it was easier when he wasn't. Not that he was ever confrontational or rude towards her, but his closed-off politeness was somehow even worse.

"So, what have we got?" she asked.

"Nine-nine-nine call came in at three thirty-four this morning," Sergeant Parsons said. "Neighbour called in the sound of a single gunshot. They said they thought it was a car backfiring at first, or maybe a firework, but then the screaming started. By the time responding officers arrived, it was clear which house the gunshot had come from. The victim's partner was still screaming. Officers gained entry at three fifty-one and found the victim, who's been identified as forty-six-year-old Darren Blanton, dead, apparently from a single gunshot wound, with fifty-three-year-old Victoria Nestell, kneeling over him and screaming."

"Any sign of the murder weapon?"

They were right on the River Thames here. It was a good place for someone to get rid of a gun. She hoped they weren't going to have to send divers into the water. That got expensive.

"Not yet, though we haven't had the chance to search the local area yet." He lifted his gaze to the sky. "Plus, it's not going to get light for a few hours yet."

The dark days were certainly upon them. Summer already felt like it had been a long time ago, even though they'd had a warm September. It was going to be a long winter, and it wasn't one Erica was looking forward to.

Though it wasn't much past four a.m., no one would be sleeping again tonight. These first few hours after an incident were the most important. Witnesses' memories could easily become foggy further down the line, and something that stood out now could quickly be forgotten. Those little things were often the key to cracking a case.

Responding officers had blocked off the street from either end. The lights were on in surrounding homes, curtains twitching, and faces pressed against the inside of the glass. It wasn't only the activity on the street that had woken them. Some may have been woken by the gunshot, while others had been awakened by uniformed police going door to door, speaking to the neighbours and trying to find out if anyone had seen or heard anything. Unfortunately, at this time in the morning, most people were tucked up in bed, but they might get lucky.

Erica checked her notes. "And who is Victoria Nestell to the victim?"

"His partner...or girlfriend...I'm not completely sure

what they refer to themselves. She was in the house when the murder happened."

"Did she see anything?"

"Unfortunately not." His line of sight moved to the light that was still on in the window of the third storey of the house. "She was upstairs in the bedroom when she heard the gunshot."

"Any signs of forced entry?"

"No. Appears as though they walked right in."

Erica raised an eyebrow. "The door wasn't locked?"

"Or the person had a key. Seems the killer ran as soon as the first shot was fired."

Erica considered the small amount of information she had so far. "Is this a burglary that was disturbed and went wrong, or did someone deliberately enter the house with the plan to kill Darren Blanton? What do we know about the victim?"

"Not much yet. He doesn't have any prior records. To be honest, there doesn't seem to be a lot on him at all."

"What about Victoria Nestell?"

"Again, no history. To the outside world, they seem like a respectable couple."

Perhaps that was exactly what they were, but Erica knew from past experience never to make assumptions or take anything at face value. It was very rare that people were who they made out to be deep down.

"We've got several security cameras around here," the sergeant continued. "Let's hope one of them caught something—someone entering the property or even fleeing the house. No one we've spoken to has reported hearing or seeing a car at that time, so we think they might have been on foot, though we don't know for sure. Hopefully,

CCTV footage will help us confirm that one way or the other."

"We might get lucky," she said. "Shall we take a look at the scene?"

"Absolutely. This way."

Erica pulled on the rest of her protective outerwear and ducked beneath the inner cordon, following the sergeant. The front door of the house already stood open, though it was being protected by a privacy tent. As soon as she stepped through, she could see why.

The front door opened onto an entrance hall, and the stairs to the next floor were directly ahead. The victim lay at the bottom of the stairs, facedown. He wore only a pair of grey boxer shorts that were now stained dark with blood. Much of his back was covered in blood, too, the source of which was the single gunshot wound right at the base of his neck.

The metallic tang of blood lay heavy on the air, intermingling with some kind of almost chemical fragrance which she put down to the plug-in on the wall that was supposed to make a person's home smell nice. She doubted the inventors of the item ever thought their fragrance would have to combat the stench of death.

Scenes of Crime Officers in white protective gear moved around the body, placing down markers and taking photographs. She ducked her head in a greeting, and they moved out of the way, giving her room to assess the crime scene for herself.

"Bastard got him from behind," the sergeant said.

Erica dropped to a crouch to study the body closer.

"Was the light on when the responding officers arrived?" she asked, glancing up at the spotlight lighting above head.

"No, it was in darkness."

Had the killer known who they were shooting? Why hadn't the victim put the light on before coming down the stairs?

Sergeant Parsons adjusted his gloves. "We're assuming one shooter, but they might not have been alone."

"Good point." Erica nodded. "Has anything been taken from the house?"

"Not that we've discovered so far, but even if it hasn't, there's a chance the intruder was disturbed before they got the chance to take anything."

This was a street that screamed money. From the expensive cars parked outside, to the three-storey, detached properties, a chancer might have hoped they'd been able to steal a couple of decent laptops or maybe even grab the keys for the Range Rover on the driveway.

Movement came from the front door, and she twisted around to find her DS entering the property.

"Morning, boss," Shawn said, not quite meeting her eye. "What's the story?"

She rose to her feet to fill him in on what she knew so far, which wasn't much.

"Break-in gone wrong?" he suggested.

"Looks that way, on the surface at least."

Shawn dropped to a crouch, the same pose Erica had been in moments earlier, to inspect the body. He paid particular attention to the hands and arms, and feet and legs.

"Doesn't seem to have been any sign of a struggle."

Erica twisted her lips. "I noticed the same."

If there had been a fight, there might have been a chance of them getting a DNA swab from beneath the victim's nails. They'd try anyway, but she wasn't holding much hope.

"Isn't it unusual for someone committing a break-in to carry a gun?" Shawn said.

The streets were getting rougher every day, with gun crime on the increase. This wasn't where she normally expected to see gun crime taking place, however. It was normally linked to gangs and organised crime, involving drugs and money.

What if there was more to this case than appeared at first glance? She made a mental note to check into the victim's background. Perhaps this nice house had been paid for by something darker than old-fashioned hard work.

She checked the body again, this time for any exit wound. There was none, which meant the bullet was most likely lodged in the victim's spine. There had only been a report of one gunshot, and there was no sign of any other bullets in the body or the surrounding area.

"We'll get ballistics on the bullet," she replied, "see if we can get a match to a weapon. We'll need to do a search of all the streets surrounding this area, including the parks and bins, in case the shooter has dumped the gun, which I imagine they would have."

Sergeant Parsons cleared his throat. "I've got some of my officers already searching, but we're definitely going to need to widen the search area."

"The victim must have seen the intruder's face," Shawn mused. "Why else shoot him when they could have just run?"

She remembered the spotlights above them. "But it was dark when the responding officers arrived. How much would he even have seen?"

"Enough to give a description."

"Turning a simple break and enter into a murder case isn't the brightest of decisions."

"Sometimes people just panic."

Erica left the body to look around the rest of the house.

As far as a murder scene went, this was a surprisingly clean one. There didn't appear to be any wounds on the victim's body, other than the single gunshot to the lower part of his neck. The area around the body, other than blood, also seemed remarkably clean. Nothing had been broken or tipped over. No drawers ransacked or windows smashed. No obvious footprints in the blood.

Other than the presence of the dead body, the house was beautifully decorated and maintained. This was clearly a well-to-do couple. Was that the reason someone had decided to target the house? They'd spotted the expensive car in the driveway and figured it would be an easy target, only to be disturbed before they got the chance to steal anything.

On the mantelpiece was a framed photograph of the couple, cheek to cheek, in that 'camera held high' position of a selfie. They seemed happy, but then who put unhappy photographs in frames for everyone to see?

She studied the victim's smiling face. It was good for her to see him like this. It reminded her that he wasn't just a body or a victim, but had been a living person with dreams and a future, only to have had it snatched away in a split second.

She returned to where Shawn and Sergeant Parsons were waiting with the body.

"Where is the victim's partner?" she asked Parsons.

"At a neighbour's house. She's extremely distressed."

"I'll need to talk to her."

"I'll go and speak to the neighbour who placed the nine-nine-nine call," Shawn said. "See if they can remember anything else that can help."

"Okay, thanks."

They went their separate ways.

THREE

Erica found Victoria Nestell sitting on a sofa in the house next door, an untouched cup of tea on the coffee table in front of her.

The home was decorated in a similar way to the house next door—all grey and beige, with furniture from Marks and Spencer, and Next, and candles artfully placed around the fireplace. There was barely a cushion out of place. Erica thought of her own home, which seemed to constantly have crumbs on the kitchen counters and shoes lying around everywhere.

A family liaison officer was sitting with Victoria, and a uniformed officer had let Erica into the house and introduced her to the neighbours, Alice and Morris Cooper. Mr Cooper quickly made himself scarce, and Alice gestured for Erica to take a seat on the wingback armchair in the corner.

Erica wondered how well the two couples knew each other. Were they the type of neighbours who invited each other around for drinks or to barbecues? Or did they simply exist, side by side, only nodding hellos at each other upon passing? Or perhaps they were the kind who despised each other, though she doubted Victoria would be sitting on the other woman's sofa right now if that was the case. She made a mental note to make sure the other officers asked these questions of the Coopers when they were no longer in hearing distance of their neighbour.

Victoria was in her fifties, and, from the smoothness of her forehead, despite her distress, looked like she'd had some work done. A fluffy dressing gown was wrapped around her slim frame, and a pair of UGG slippers were on her feet.

"Mrs Nestell?" Erica enquired.

"It's Ms now." She sniffed, her voice strangled. "But call me Vicki."

"I'm DI Swift, the investigating officer on your partner's case. I understand this is very difficult for you, but do you think you might be able to answer some questions for me? The first few hours after an incident like this are the most important."

Victoria hitched a breath. "I-I don't know what I can tell you. I didn't see anything."

Erica offered her a reassuring smile. "Let's start at the beginning. Did anything happen yesterday that stands out in your mind as being unusual? Did you see anyone hanging around the house, for example? Any strange phone calls or run-ins with anyone?"

People's motivations could be hard to decipher. Maybe the couple were victims of a road-rage incident, and someone followed them home to take their revenge? While this appeared to be a burglary gone wrong on the surface, Erica had enough experience to know it was always important to dig deeper.

Vicki blinked, fresh tears rolling down her cheeks. "No, nothing like that. It was just a regular day."

"Okay. Tell me about last night. Did you go to bed as normal?"

"Yes. We'd shared a bottle of red wine in front of the television, then Darren went up before me, but he often does. He's more of an early riser than I am—" Her voice broke. "I mean, he *was* more of an early riser. He went up to bed shortly after eleven, and I went to bed about midnight. He was already asleep when I went up."

"And then what happened?" Erica prompted.

"I woke up during the night, but, at first, I didn't know what had woken me. Then I heard something downstairs, and I just knew someone else was in the house." She pressed her lips into a line, so they almost disappeared, and her chin trembled.

"It's okay, take your time," Erica said gently.

The other woman sniffed again and nodded.

Erica gave her a moment and then continued. "So you heard a noise. Do you know what that noise was?"

"No, I was half asleep. I think it must have been the front or back door opening, but honestly, I'm guessing. I just woke up with the certainty of someone being downstairs, and as soon as I saw that Darren was still beside me in bed, I got this rush of adrenaline and woke him up, too."

"You didn't think to call nine-nine-nine right away?"

She wiped away her tears. "God, of course I wish I had, but maybe I didn't completely believe myself either. I only wanted a bit of reassurance so I could go back to sleep. I'd give anything to have done something differently now."

"So how long after he went downstairs did you hear the gunshot?"

"Less than a minute. It was almost right away."

"And what did you do then?"

Victoria paused, chewing on her lower lip. "I hate to say it, but I froze. I was like a little kid, hiding under the bedcovers. I was terrified the gunman was going to come upstairs, that he'd know I was there, and decide to shoot me, too."

Erica linked her fingers between her knees. "The nine-nine-nine call we received was from a neighbour. Why didn't you call the police?"

"It sounds stupid, but I didn't think of it. When no one came up to shoot me, too, all I could think about was Darren. I only wanted to go to him and make sure he was all right." She choked again. "He wasn't."

The responding officers had entered the property to find Vicki crying over the top of her dead boyfriend, holding his head in her lap and rocking back and forth. They'd struggled to get any information at all out of her at first, she was so distressed. They hadn't needed to break into the house to gain entry. The doors had already been unlocked.

"I'm so sorry," Erica said. "How did the two of you meet?"

She gave a strange sound which might have been a laugh. "Online. It's such a cliché, isn't it? But then everyone is meeting that way these days. We haven't been together long. Only eight months. I thought we were going to grow old together, though. We were serious about each other."

"Is the house jointly owned?"

Victoria shook her head. "No, it's my house. I lost my

husband five years ago to a heart attack. I'd bought the house with him, years ago. Darren moved in a couple of months after we met." She swiped tears away from her cheeks with the backs of her knuckles. "I can't believe I've lost him, too. God, why is life so unfair?" She broke down into sobs.

"I realise this is extremely difficult for you. Is there any reason you can think of that someone might have wanted to hurt Darren?"

She lifted her head and blinked. "What do you mean? This was a burglary, wasn't it?"

Erica was careful about how she phrased things, not wanting to worry the other woman unnecessarily. "Most likely, yes, but so far, we can't tell that anything was taken."

"Because poor Darren disturbed them. That was my fault. I was the one who told him to go downstairs. I was the one who forgot to lock the doors last night. It's all my fault."

She trembled all over, chewing at the edges of her fake nails. She reminded Erica of one of those bald, crested dogs that always looked like it had anxiety issues.

"Does he have any family?" Erica asked. "Any next of kin we need to notify?"

"His family all live abroad. Spain, I think. I've never met them."

Erica angled her head. "Family as in parents?"

"Yes. He doesn't have any siblings that I'm aware of."

Erica considered this. "Would he have their contact details on his phone or laptop?"

"Possibly, but I think they were estranged. I guess they'd still want to know. His phone and laptop must still be in the house, assuming they weren't stolen, but I don't know his password or anything like that. You're welcome to take them, if they'll help."

"Thank you. What about friends? Work colleagues."

"He's an entrepreneur. Deals in property, mainly, so he doesn't really have colleagues. I believe he's between properties right now, though."

"What about yourself? What do you do for a living?"

"Oh, I'm semi-retired now. I owned my own marketing company but sold it twelve months ago. I still do consultations, but that's all."

Erica wondered just how much she'd sold the company for. Had money been a motive in this murder?

Darren had been a good few years younger than Victoria, and it looked like she was the person who'd brought the house and money to the table. Had she paid for the expensive vehicle on the driveway as well? Erica didn't like to make judgements, but that was part of her job.

But then Erica reminded herself that she'd been a few years older than Shawn, too. She'd also been the person who owned the house after her husband had died. It didn't mean that Shawn was gold-digging—he'd have thought the possibility hilarious—but would people have thought the same about them? Not that it mattered now. Their relationship was over, at least in a romantic sense. They were doing their utmost to keep things purely professional, especially so their history didn't impact the rest of the team, but it wasn't easy. They'd lost that comfortable camaraderie between them. The pain they'd both gone through was like a taut thread that forever joined them. She wasn't sure she'd ever get over it.

She'd gone through a lot of soul searching over the past few months. For some time, she found herself angry at the poor, unborn baby she'd lost. If only she'd never fallen pregnant, only to lose the baby, the relationship wouldn't have failed. But she also knew that the pregnancy was a catalyst for something that had run deeper—something she'd always feared—that Shawn was young enough to still want a family of his own. Though she loved him, she wasn't going to be the one to stand in his way of that happening.

"Okay, well, if you can think of anyone, please let me know. I appreciate you taking the time to talk to me. I realise it hasn't been easy. I am truly sorry for your loss." She handed the grieving woman her card. "We will probably need to speak with you again, but if there is anything else you think of in the meantime, please give me a call. Any time. No matter how small you think it might be, it could be something important." She paused and then added, "Do you have any family we can call for you?

"My son. He's already on his way."

"Will you be able to stay with him for a few days? The house is a crime scene now, so I'm afraid we won't be able to let you back in until we've processed it. I can get one of my officers to collect a change of clothes and some toiletries for you."

"Yes, thank you. I can stay with him." She gave a cold, strange kind of laugh. "He never did approve of Darren."

FOUR

A couple of hours later, Erica and Shawn were back in the office.

Erica turned to the board attached to the wall of the incident room. She nursed a cup of hot coffee, while studying what she'd pinned up so far. On the board was a map of the area where the murder house was located. Photographs of the crime scene, and of the victim's body, plus the markers that had been placed around the area, were also attached. Another set of pictures showed the blood spatter from where the victim had been shot. Analysing it would give them a good idea of the exact positions of the shooter and the victim the moment the bullet was fired.

She took another sip of her coffee. It had been a very early start, and she was going to need to mainline this stuff if she was going to get through the day.

Her team started filing in, chatting among one another and finding places to sit.

Now Hannah Rudd had left to join a different team

as a detective sergeant, the office was feeling very testosterone heavy. Erica had grown to like her new member, DC Lewis Crowe, though. He'd fitted in well, and though he'd been nervous to start, now he'd relaxed, he was bringing in a little light relief to the group. She missed having another female presence around, though, and missed Hannah, too. They'd worked together for a long time, and Erica admired and respected the younger woman. She wished her well on her new challenge.

Things were still tense with Shawn, but she was grateful he hadn't transferred out of her team. There had been several weeks where she was certain she'd be notified that she was getting a new detective sergeant, but that hadn't happened.

He was still in her life, and that was the most important thing. Actually, the most important thing was that he was still in Poppy's life, too. Poppy had only been tiny when her father had been murdered, and Shawn was the closest thing to a dad that Poppy had ever really known, or at least could remember. It had felt unbearably cruel to take him out of her life as well.

Erica's thoughts lingered on her daughter.

Things hadn't been easy for Poppy. She'd started her new secondary school—which they all now referred to as high school in that annoying way that everyone seemed to adopt certain 'Americanisms' for things. Erica blamed YouTube. The few friends Poppy had from primary school had quickly gone off with new friends, leaving Poppy alone. Erica had done her best to encourage her daughter to branch out as well, and try to speak to new people, but it wasn't easy. Then she found out that Poppy had the wrong kind of bag for school—one that was apparently uncool among the preteens—which had led to teasing and Poppy feeling even more insecure than ever.

Add that to the heartbreak over Erica losing the baby, and then Shawn leaving, and it had all been too much for poor Poppy. Erica hated to see her struggling but felt completely helpless when it came to knowing what was the right thing to do.

Her boss, DCI Gibbs, also came into the room and found a seat at the back. He winced as he sat, and then rubbed at a spot at the base of his neck. He was looking older. It reminded Erica that nothing ever stayed the same, however much she might want it to.

She cleared her throat, drawing the attention of her team.

"Morning, everyone. Let's get started." The general chatter died down as attention was focused to the front of the room. "Shortly after three-thirty this morning, forty-six-year-old Darren Blanton was shot at his home. His partner, Victoria Nestell, was upstairs at the time, but it was one of the neighbours who placed the emergency call. So far, there's no sign of the gun that was used in the shooting." She gestured to the map and the property that had been marked out on it. "The road the house is located on is only one street away from the River Thames. We have local police searching the area. My best guess is that the perpetrator will have wanted to get rid of the weapon as soon as possible, and we might need to consider that they'll have tossed it in the river."

She glanced towards the back to where DCI Gibbs was sitting. She already knew he'd be mentally calculating the costs of bringing divers in.

"This is a clean crime scene, but hopefully we'll get

something from it," she continued. "We've got SOCO printing the scene, but if the intruder was wearing gloves, which, considering they also had the foresight to take a gun with them, they most likely were, we might not get anything."

"How did the shooter gain entry to the house?" DC Crowe asked.

Erica exhaled a breath. "Currently, it looks like they walked right in. Victoria believes there's a strong possibility that she didn't lock the doors that evening. She said she and Darren had shared a bottle of red wine, and she thought he'd already done it and didn't bother to check. She's blaming herself, of course. If the doors had been locked, perhaps there would have been a very different outcome."

"So it could have been a gang trying their luck?" DC Jon Howard said from where he was sitting. "Going door to door until they found one that was open?"

Erica nodded. "That is a possibility, yes. We'll interview people living in the surrounding streets as well, see if anyone saw or heard any disturbances or if someone had security cameras that might have picked up on a gang trying the doors." She thought of something else. "Let's check for any recent break-ins or attempted break-ins in the local area, say over the past three months. It might be that this isn't the first time the culprit has broken into someone's house. They could be a serial offender, this is just the first time they've been disturbed. If we didn't catch the offender or offenders on CCTV this time around, maybe we caught them during a previous crime. They could be someone known to us."

Erica paused to take a sip of her coffee and gather her thoughts to make sure she was on the right path. "We have a few neighbours who heard the gunshot, though most believed it to be something else like a car backfiring or a firework. The timings they gave match up with that reported by the only real witness—the victim's partner, Victoria Nestell. Like several in the area, the property is spread over three floors, with the master bedroom being on the top floor, so while she heard the gunshot, by the time she got downstairs, the shooter was long gone, and unfortunately, so was the victim. It's thought he died moments after the shooting, though we'll know more after the post-mortem."

A murmur of remorse went around the room, and she allowed a beat to pass out of respect for the victim before she continued.

"The positive to take from this is that we have an exact time that the shooter fled from the property, which will make tracking them down on CCTV that much easier. Because it doesn't look as though they took anything from the property, I don't believe they were inside the house for long either before they were disturbed. That gives us a very narrow time where we can check all local CCTV, plus trace every vehicle that was on the road in that same area at that time." She lifted her chin to give out actions to her team. "DC Howard, can you follow up on the CCTV? Make sure we've located all the possible cameras and got the footage."

"Sure thing, boss."

She thought of something else. "Check all the cars parked on the street as well, marry them up with all the local residents."

He tapped his fingers to his forehead in a salute.

"We haven't yet notified the victim's next of kin. According to his partner, he has parents in Spain, but she

hasn't given us any contact details or even their names. .
We'll have to loop back around with Victoria Nestell and
see if there's anything in the home that might have their
details—an old letter, perhaps, or we might find a phone
number or email address on the victim's phone or laptop.
Let's make sure the press don't release his name until
we've had the chance to notify the next of kin."

She focused on her newest team member, DC Crowe.
"Lewis, can you request the victim's phone and bank
records, see if anything comes up as being unusual? The
victim's partner was happy for us to seize his laptop and
phone, too, though she didn't have any clue what his pass-
words might be, so they're with digital forensics now.
Maybe this is just a simple break-in that went wrong, but
if there's a chance it isn't, I want to know about it."

She took a couple of paces and turned her attention to
her partner. Even saying his name sent adrenaline
through her veins, but she did her best to keep her voice
level. She didn't want him to see that he affected her. She
tried to stay professional at all times.

"Shawn, can you liaise with the search team and
gather the statements from the neighbours? Make sure
we're on top of any developments that officers at the scene
might make."

He didn't meet her eye. "No problem."

"Let's look into the victim as well. I'm not entirely
sure what the setup is there, but something tells me something is off. He hasn't lived there for long and doesn't have
a regular job. Was he in trouble of any kind? Did he have
any money or drug problems? His partner says not, but it
might be that she doesn't know him as well as she thinks.
They've only been together eight months."

He nodded. "Sure."

She looked around again, addressing everyone. "There are a number of questions we need to ask ourselves. How did the shooter get to and from the house? Did they walk, or was there a mode of transport involved? Were they alone, or did they have an accomplice?"

At this stage of an investigation, there were so many different avenues they could go down. Erica often felt like it was similar to casting out a wide net and hauling in whatever information they could. It was impossible to know which tiny detail might be the one that led them to a conviction, so she had to make sure she had everything.

"We're going to need to get Victoria to take a better look around once SOCO have finished with the crime scene, check nothing was taken from the house. We're also waiting on the post-mortem results, results from forensics, and, assuming we can retrieve the bullet, from ballistics as well. It's going to be at least a couple of days before any of that comes in, so we're going to have to work with what we have.

"I don't have to tell you all that these next twenty-four hours are critical to the investigation, so I want you all to make finding the shooter the top of your priorities. Thank you, everyone."

Her team gathered their belongings and paperwork, clearing their throats and exiting the room. Shawn was last to leave, but before he did, something else occurred to her.

"One second, Shawn." She stopped him. "I'm reaching, but Victoria made an offhand comment about how her son didn't approve of Darren. Victoria sold her company recently. I imagine a son, who expects to inherit that money when his mother eventually passes, wouldn't be too happy about a younger man moving in and potentially laying claim on his inheritance."

"You think he'd go as far as killing off the rival?"

"Money is an excellent motivator. The son's name is Justin Nestell."

Shawn fixed his gaze on hers and gave her a curt nod. "I'll dig into his background."

FIVE

Neve Carter sat behind her desk in her corner office, staring down at the new profile picture her daughter had taken for her on her phone, and grimaced.

She didn't really look like that, did she? In her head, she was still in her twenties, or at the most, her thirties, but then she saw a photograph of herself at the grand age of fifty-one, and she struggled to recognise herself.

It wasn't that she was bad for her age. In fact, she thought she kept herself looking well. She always invested in expensive face creams, had her hair done, kept herself trim, and made sure to balance that line with her clothing so that they were neither frumpy nor mutton dressed as lamb.

She sighed. It wasn't easy being a woman of a certain age. Maybe she'd feel differently if she was still married, but she wasn't, so that was that. Her daughter was twenty now, and how envious Neve was of her youth. She knew she needed to get over it, but when it seemed like all the men who were her age only wanted to date thirty-year-olds, she couldn't help but be bitter. The worst part was that thirty-year-olds were dating them! She blamed the whole 'silver fox' thing for making older men more attractive.

She gave herself a shake. She was a successful, professional woman. While her job wasn't the most exciting in the world—she managed a finance team that dealt with complaints—she was on a good salary, especially for London. She'd raised a daughter and owned her home outright now. In her Reiss trouser suit, and with both designer shoes and handbag, she tried to dress well. She drove an Audi A4, which admittedly was on hire purchase, and was probably a bit of an unnecessary luxury since it wasn't worth driving into work because the parking charges were extortionate. But even so, she didn't think she was doing too badly for herself.

She just had one part of her life that was missing.

She was lonely.

Neve tossed her phone to one side and forced herself to focus on her work. On the other side of the glass that made up the walls of her office, rows of cubby-hole desks ran one after the other, creating an seemingly endless sea of heads of the telephone operators who ran them. The place was filled with a constant stream of chatter that sometimes reminded her of the buzz of a distant motorway. When she'd first started here, she'd thought she'd never be able to concentrate, that the noise was always going to be distracting, but now she barely noticed it. It was easy to zone things out after a while, and she'd been working here for going on ten years now.

She left her desk to do the rounds of the office, checking if anyone needed help, or if anyone was playing games on their phone rather than working. Plenty of people stopped her, asking questions about certain policies, or simply enquiring whether their holiday request had been granted yet.

Barely an hour had passed when a notification popped up on her phone. *<Guy wants to make a connection.>*

It was from one of the dating apps she subscribed to. Neve hesitated and then clicked the link.

The photograph was of a man with a thick head of silvery hair and clear blue eyes who seemed to be about her age. His smile was warm and genuine, as though he'd just been laughing at something someone off camera had just said, the corners of his eyes crinkling.

He even had all his own teeth.

She wasn't about to start jumping for joy, however. She'd been here before. How many men had she thought were good-looking from their profile pictures, only to turn up to meet them for a date to discover the photo must have been taken twenty years ago and that they'd definitely lied about their ages. That was for the ones who weren't obvious scammers. She'd long ago learned to do a reverse image search on Google to see if they'd stolen their profile picture from an online site. It was amazing how many doctors living abroad seemed to be wanting to date her.

Neve stared down at the photograph. He was attractive, but not too attractive, which always raised red flags in her mind. Of course, with the use of AI these days, it wasn't always easy to tell.

"Ooh, he's cute," a female voice said from over her shoulder.

It was her colleague, Lacey. She was another one of the managers here, though she'd not been here anywhere near as long as Neve and wasn't quite as high in the ranks. Her desk was still in amongst all the other office workers rather than in a separate space.

"If he's even real. He's probably an AI scam artist."

"You can't think that about everyone."

"Okay then, he's probably about seventy years old and this picture was taken in the early two thousands."

"How will you know if you don't meet him?"

A sigh fell from her lips. "This all just feels like a huge waste of time. I miss the days when I could go and get drunk in a bar and just meet someone there."

She'd done exactly that with her ex-husband, and look how that had turned out? While she didn't regret their fifteen years together, especially as it had resulted in her daughter, Chloe, she did feel bitter about never getting her happily ever after. Marriages were supposed to be full of ups and downs—in sickness and in health, right?—but Tim had bailed the moment he'd decided they were living more like roommates than husband and wife. She'd just thought they were having a bad patch, but he said he wanted more, and by more she assumed that meant a thirty-year-old girlfriend.

"You can still do that!" Lacey encouraged. "Plenty of people meet men in bars."

"It's easy for you to say. You're only...what...thirty-one?"

"Thirty-three," Lacey said, sounding a little offended, though Neve would have taken looking younger as a compliment.

"Well, at your age, you can still look like fun if you're drunk in a bar. Once you pass fifty, it's just sad."

Lacey nudged her with her hip. "No, it doesn't! You're just telling yourself all these things as an excuse not to do it. You should give this bloke a chance. He's local. What's the worst that could happen?"

"I end up dating a serial killer?"

Lacey rolled her eyes, a smile tugging the corners of her lips. "You're too dramatic."

"Am I? The number one killer of women is men."

"I'm not sure that's true."

Neve laughed. "Okay, maybe it's heart disease, but it sounds right."

"Just give this one a chance. You never know. He might be just what you're looking for. You're too young and beautiful to be all alone."

"You sound like my daughter."

"Well, your daughter is right. Go on. Reply to his message and say you'd like to meet for coffee." Lacey glanced over her shoulder towards one of the other offices —this one with actual walls rather than just glass. "Or you could always ask Nigel out on a date. You know how he spends half his day here gazing over wistfully at you."

Nigel Hunton was Neve's boss and also the office creep.

Neve gave a mock shudder. "Ugh, please don't."

"Neve and Nigel," she said in a sing-song voice. "I think it has a cute ring to it."

Nasty Nigel. Naughty Nigel. Noxious Nigel... The list went on. He was definitely not the sort of man she wanted in her future, even though he'd asked her out several times now. She'd always awkwardly refused, saying that she didn't want to mix work with pleasure, when in actual fact she'd prefer to walk over molten glass barefooted than spend the night with him. He was the sort of man who'd call a woman a bitch because she didn't appreciate his catcall, and honestly, she wasn't even sure why he was still working here. She'd thought HR would have got rid of him years ago. He acted as though Neve should be thankful he'd asked her out, while ogling the twenty-year-old office workers over her shoulder.

Neve glanced down at the screen again, her thumb hovering over the top of the message. What was the point of being on these dating apps if she wasn't ever going to give any of the potential daters a go? She'd never have admitted it out loud, preferring instead to say she was comfortable with her own company, but she missed having someone to share her evenings with. It didn't help that with social media, she was constantly bombarded with all the wonderful lives everyone else was leading. She'd tried not to check, but then she felt even worse. At least social media gave her a bit of a connection to other people.

She blew out a breath. "Okay, fine, I'll do it."

Lacey punched the air. "Yes, atta girl."

Quickly, Neve typed out a reply.

To her surprise, an answer came right away.

<What are you doing later?>

<Not much.>

<Six p.m. at La Trattoria? Though I might have a beer rather than a coffee.>

He ended the message with a winky face, and she found herself smiling.

"Guess I have a date," she said to Lacey.

"See!" Lacey practically squealed. "I told you so."

She suddenly realised she would have to meet him wearing the white blouse and boring navy-blue trousers she'd worn to work. "Shit. I can't go dressed like this. And I don't even have any makeup with me."

"We'll head out at lunch," Lacey reassured her. "Shop

for something hot and stop by one of the department stores for the makeup counter to give you a makeover."

"Then I'll feel obliged to buy something."

"So buy something. Treat yourself. You deserve it."

Yes, maybe she did, she thought.

SIX

The morning flew by.

Erica found herself lost in a sea of phone calls and emails. The volume of information gathering at this early stage of an investigation was always huge. She trusted her team to have a handle on the majority of it, but there were always things that ended up on her plate, plus she still had paperwork from prior investigations to juggle. They didn't just disappear because a new case had landed in her lap.

After lunch—which was a sandwich she'd grabbed from the local coffee shop and eaten in front of her computer—Lewis Crowe approached Erica's desk.

"Boss, I've located all the cameras from the local area. Do you want the good news or the bad news?"

She pulled a face. "Let's start with the good news."

"There are six cameras in the local vicinity."

"That is good news...and the bad news?"

"Nobody's camera works." He gave a small shrug. "Well, or variations on that theme. One camera wasn't charged, another only captures live recordings because they don't want to pay for the recording. Another camera is fake, they just use it as a preventative to stop people coming onto their property. Someone else says their camera was already there when they bought the house and they don't even know how it works. Which leaves only two working cameras. Now one is pointing the wrong way, but there's still a chance they might have caught the shooter walking past, and the other one is pointing the right way, but they can't remember their password to access their footage, and so they've requested to reset it. I'm still waiting to hear back from them."

"A productive morning then?" she teased.

"Very. There's still a chance the final camera will show something, but I'm not holding my breath."

It was disappointing that the cameras hadn't come up with anything useful yet, but she wasn't surprised. While people might complain about the use of CCTV, in her experience, the chance of actually catching a crime happening directly on camera was still slim. It wasn't even that criminals had got wise to them. It was more that no one bothered to keep the damn things working.

"What about the vehicles parked in the street?" she asked. "Anything jump out as being unusual?"

"I haven't had the chance to check them all yet, but I'll get onto it."

"Okay, thanks, Lewis."

He walked away, and she stifled a yawn and rubbed beneath her eyes with her index finger. It had been a painfully early start, and she hadn't even seen her daughter that morning.

At least with Poppy being that little bit older now, she got to see her in the evenings more. She remembered when Poppy had been a baby and a toddler, and how it had hurt every time she'd arrived home too late to give her a bath or put her to bed. There had been times where she'd wondered if Poppy had even known she was her mother, or if Poppy had wondered in her tiny baby head who this strange woman was who randomly appeared in her bedroom during the night.

She couldn't decide if she was relieved or saddened by the fact her daughter was no longer at primary school. Normally, at this time of year, she'd be preparing for the barrage of Christmas shows, and school fayres, and breakfasts with Santa, and expectations to bake cakes and donate items for raffles. It was something she'd been increasingly frustrated with over the years. But now there was nothing like that going on. No cute nativity play with the donkey falling off the stage and one of the shepherds crying or picking his nose at the back. The most the secondary school was doing was a Christmas lunch that the kids could choose not to partake in, if they didn't want to, and a Christmas jumper day—which was also not mandatory. She couldn't imagine many teens or preteens would willingly dress themselves up in an ugly jumper in order to be teased by their friends.

Maybe she should have appreciated those times a little more instead of being frustrated by them. But it had been hard, especially when Poppy had been doing something like having a part in a play, and Erica hadn't been able to get there because of work. She'd always felt like such a failure as a mother, particularly as Poppy didn't have a dad to fill in that place either.

Now those times were over, and maybe Erica should be relieved, but instead she had a sense of loss sitting as a heavy weight in her chest.

From across the other side of the office, DC Jon

Howard caught her attention. "I've found something, boss."

Erica rose from her seat to join him at his computer. "What have you got?"

"I've been looking into crime reports in the area over the past few months, and there was an attempted break-in of a house a couple of streets away from the shooting."

"When did this happen?"

He picked up a pen, tapping it against his thigh. "Two weeks ago. The homeowner heard someone trying to break the lock."

"What did they do?"

He gave a small laugh. "Opened the door and chased the intruders away with a baseball bat."

Her eyebrows shot up. "Seriously?"

"Yeah. They picked on the wrong house. It was only after they'd left that the resident called the police, and even then, they only called one-oh-one as they didn't believe it was an emergency."

"I think I might want to talk to this person."

Jon sat back in his chair and grinned. "I'm sure that can be arranged."

SEVEN

The house where the previous break-in had taken place was only about ten minutes on foot away from the scene of the murder. There was a stronger police presence around the area, with both search teams and teams of uniformed officers going door to door, asking questions as to whether anyone had seen or heard anything.

Since he was the one who'd learned of the preceding crime, Erica had brought DC Howard with her to speak to the baseball-bat-wielding resident.

Though it was in close proximity, the actual street was very different to the one where Darren Blanton had been murdered. Where those homes were all three-storey townhouses, these properties were small council houses, or ex-council houses with brown cladding, and neighbours attached on both sides. If it was the same person or persons responsible for the break-in, they'd certainly gone for an upgrade.

She made a mental note to check if any of the neighbours here had seen or heard anything the night of the attempted break-in. They must have been aware of a disturbance if this man had chased people down the road with a bat.

Erica approached the front door, Jon following close behind her, and rang the bell.

The man who opened the door was approximately six foot two, with a long beard that covered the lower part of his face. He was in his early fifties, a band t-shirt stretched across his muscled chest. She suddenly understood why he'd felt capable of taking on whoever had been trying to break into his house, though it wouldn't have mattered how big he'd been if he'd come face to face with a gun like Darren Blanton had.

"Mr Whittle? Russel Whittle? I'm DI Swift, and this is my colleague, DC Howard. We'd like to talk to you about an attempted break-in you had a couple of weeks ago."

His face furrowed in a frown. "I already spoke to someone when it happened."

"I understand that, but I'm sure you've heard about the shooting that happened last night. There's a possibility the two cases are connected."

He scrubbed at his beard with his right hand and stepped back. "Guess you'd better come in then."

He was clearly reluctant to be speaking to them, but he let them in and then gestured towards a door on the left, indicating for them to go through. They did just that, and Erica found herself in a small but tidy living room.

Russel Whittle followed them in. "You might as well sit down."

Erica and Jon sat side by side on the sofa, while the occupant of the house slumped down into a recliner chair.

"Do you live alone, Mr Whittle?" Erica asked.

"Cut the 'Mr Whittle' shit out. My name is Russ. And yeah, I live alone."

Erica checked her notes. "You reported an attempted break-in on the thirteenth of November? Is that right?"

"Yeah, but only after I'd given the people who'd tried to get into my home a run for their money. Those little pricks chose the wrong house to try to break into."

"By 'run for their money', are you referencing the way you chased them from the house with a baseball bat?"

Russel Whittle didn't seem like the type of person who would have any interest in baseball. She had no doubt that the item was kept at the house for exactly this kind of incident.

"Yeah, I am."

"You should have called nine-nine-nine right away. We might have caught them then."

He shrugged. "Unlikely. By the time your lot would have arrived, they'd have been long gone."

"Perhaps," she said noncommittally. "But they might not have been, and if these were the same people responsible for the shooting last night, they might just have saved a life."

"Anyway, I'm not a fan of the police." He sniffed. "Done some time years back. I prefer to handle things myself."

"But you did call the police," she added, "eventually."

"Yeah. I didn't want them breaking into some little old lady's home and scaring her half to death. I thought I'd given them enough of a fright, but then after I thought it over some, I figured they might have just regrouped and be trying somewhere else."

"What time was it when you heard them trying to break in?"

"Just after two in the morning."

A similar time to the shooting. "And where were you at the time?"

"Just sitting on my sofa, watching Netflix. I'm more of a night owl, but I had the blinds down, so I guess they didn't see the light from the television or they'd have known someone was up. I recognised the noise for what it was right away. Like I said, I have a...colourful...past. They definitely chose the wrong house to try."

"Do you have cameras?"

"Nah, I don't trust them. Too many bloody CCTV cameras around as it is. I don't plan on adding to them. You can't even walk down the street in London without someone watching you on camera. It's an invasion of privacy."

She wanted to tell him it was a matter of people's safety but knew there was no point arguing. People had generally made up their own minds about these things, and there was no changing them, unless, of course, they had a reason to need the footage from a street camera themselves. Then, she found, they often had a change of heart.

"Can you give me a description of the people breaking in?"

Beside her, Jon took out his notepad to jot down what Mr Whittle was saying.

"There were three of them, that I saw anyway. There might have been more, and one just took off before the others or was hiding somewhere. They were all wearing black and had masks covering the lower part of their faces, and hoodies pulled up to cover their hair. They had definitely set out to cause some trouble. They'd planned for it."

"Were they on foot, or did they have a vehicle?"

He sighed heavily. "You know, I told all of this to the person I spoke to when I called the police."

"I know, but with the shooting not far from here, you might have a different viewpoint on things now, or we might have a new angle that we need to ask questions from. We won't take up too much more of your time," she reassured him.

"They were young," he continued, "or at least that's the impression I got of them."

"Did you get a look at their skin tone? Did they say anything, and did you pick up on any accents? What about any distinguishing features?"

"One of them said 'oh, fuck.' And the other said 'run.'" He chuckled at that. "Think they were local. White, too, but I might be mistaken on that. Like I said, most of their skin was covered up, and it was dark. I saw more of them running away than anything else."

"They were on foot then? You didn't see them getting into a car?"

"Nope. Didn't mean they didn't have one, though. They might have just been parked around the corner. As soon as they were off my street, I turned around and came home again. I'd left my front door wide open when I chased after them and I didn't want to give someone else the chance to steal my shit."

Erica brought up a map of the area on her phone and held it out for Russ to see. "Can you show me which direction they went in?"

He pointed at the road. "They went this way."

Towards the one decent-sized supermarket that was located on the peninsula.

She didn't know how deeply the police had investigated the case. Maybe they'd caught the culprits on camera, but no one had looked into it deeply enough to see them. After all, an attempted breaking and entering wasn't going to be top of their priority list.

There was a chance this had nothing to do with the shooting, of course. She was also conscious of not wasting time heading in the wrong direction.

"Thank you, Russ. We appreciate your help."

He shrugged, as though he didn't care too much one way or the other.

Erica left him one of her cards, asking him to contact her if he remembered anything else. She doubted that she'd hear from him, but stranger things had happened. She and Jon left the house and went back to the car.

She opened the driver's door. "Tracking down CCTV from that night seems like the best option."

"Even if they were caught on camera, you think it'll still exist after two weeks?" Jon said across the roof of the car.

Erica paused for a moment and then shrugged. "Maybe, maybe not, but it's always worth asking."

EIGHT

It was already dark when Neve arrived where she'd arranged to meet her date—a man called Guy Thurgood.

Though it wasn't late, the sun went down by four in the afternoon now, which made Neve feel as though she arrived at the office in the dark and then left in the dark, too.

A fine mist of rain had just started, and it was icy cold and threatened to turn her already terminally frizzy brown hair into a halo. A warm glow came from the windows of the pub, promising warmth and shelter from the miserable weather. She buried her nose and chin into her red scarf and shoved her hands deeper into her coat pockets.

Neve's stomach churned as she paused at the door. She hated being nervous. He was just some bloke from the internet, and she told herself that she didn't care what random men thought of her, but why did she have butterflies dancing in her belly?

Okay, so he'd seemed attractive from his photograph, but she was fully expecting him to look nothing like that picture. He'd probably be a *lot* older, and, from past experiences, chain-smoked or still lived with his mother. Those were normally the sort of things men conveniently left out of their profile information, and that was even if they bothered showing up and didn't decide to ghost her, even after being the one to initiate contact. The other fun discovery she often found out was that her date would be completely obsessed with his ex and spend the entire time talking about her. It was even worse when they spoke badly about their ex than if they said how much they missed or still loved them. She'd walked out on one date who'd called his ex-wife a bitch and a whore and said that he hoped she got her comeuppance for daring to leave him. The red flags had been waving wildly for that one.

Neve pulled open the pub door and stepped inside. At this time, it was still quiet, and she scanned the room, searching for the person she was meeting.

On the other side of the bar, a man matching the profile picture caught her eye. He locked her gaze with his, and it brightened with recognition. He lifted his hand in a half wave and hopped down from the stool where he'd been perched.

She was pleasantly surprised. He actually resembled his profile picture.

While she was happy she hadn't been stood up, she did wish she'd arrived before him. She hoped her nose wasn't too red from the cold and that her eye makeup hadn't smudged. The woman on the makeup counter in the department store had done an excellent job—and yes, Neve had felt obliged to purchase at least half the products she'd used—but with the persistent drizzle she'd had to combat on the way here, she now wished she'd jumped in a black cab instead of fighting the Tube. She desperately wanted to duck straight into the ladies' room to check out her reflection, but he'd already spotted her, and she didn't want to appear vain.

A smile spread across Neve's lips.

She wound her way between the tables to head to the bar.

"Neve," he greeted her, leaning in to plant a kiss against her cheek. "Thank you so much for agreeing to meet me on such short notice."

She offered him a smile. "Oh, you were lucky I had a break in my busy social schedule."

His expression faltered.

"I'm joking," she added hurriedly. "I most definitely don't have a busy social schedule."

"That's good, 'cause mine is completely barren." He laughed. "What can I get you to drink?"

She checked the time. It was after six p.m. But she also didn't want to be judged for drinking at this time on a Tuesday evening. Fuck it, she decided. She was an adult and could have an alcoholic drink if she wanted one.

"I'll have a glass of dry white wine, please."

"Phew. I was eyeing up a pint, but didn't want you to think I was a lush."

She found herself laughing and tucked a strand of hair behind her ear. "I was thinking the same thing. I'm glad we're on the same page."

They held each other's eye for a beat, and then he turned to the bartender and lifted a hand to get the younger man's attention. He ordered, and, once they'd got their drinks, they found a table in the corner.

"So, tell me a bit about yourself, Neve," he said after they'd sat. "What do you do for work?"

She grimaced. "It's not very exciting, I'm afraid. I'm a

manager in a call centre for a finance company. I manage a team that deals with complaints, mainly, which can be... interesting. What about yourself?"

"I run a business selling china."

"China? I assume you're not referring to the country and mean more like mugs and plates and stuff?"

He chuckled. "Yes, but not like the kind you'd find down at your local supermarket either. These are top quality—the likes of which you'll find in the equivalent to Harrods but in Saudi Arabia and Singapore."

"Oh, right. That sounds interesting."

Maybe she sounded unsure because he laughed again.

"I promise it is more interesting than it sounds. I get to travel a lot with my work and meet lots of different people. No one day is ever the same."

"So why aren't you in a relationship right now?" She decided to get straight down to business. If he was a commitment-phobe or had been married five times, she wanted to know about it.

He seemed to consider this. "Honestly, I think my work has something to do with it. Like I said before, I travel a lot, which means I'm not always around to do things like this. I guess I'm hoping to meet an independent woman who is confident in herself and doesn't mind if she has to spend a week or so alone because I have to fly to Singapore for a meeting."

"I'm used to being alone." She stopped herself, not wanting to sound pathetic. "I mean, I have my daughter and my friends, of course, but I'm comfortable in my own company."

"I think once you get to our sort of age, you kind of learn to be, don't you think?"

"Definitely," she agreed. "What about past relationships? Have you been married before? Any kids?"

"No, and no. I came close, a couple of times, but it never worked out."

Neve wasn't sure if it was a good or bad thing that he didn't have any baggage. What was wrong with him that he'd never made that leap into marriage? Did it send red flags flying?

"I know how that sounds," he continued, "but really, why do we need marriage these days anyway? Commitment should be between two people. It shouldn't need to be confirmed by a piece of paper or by the church."

Said like a classic commitment-phobe, she thought.

"I have no intention of ever getting married again," she said instead of speaking aloud her thoughts. "My last one didn't end so well, and I certainly don't ever want to put that kind of faith in 'happily ever after'. I'm not sure I believe in such a thing anymore. I'd prefer to think in terms of happy for now."

He winced. "Sounds like your ex hurt you."

"Yeah, he did. I guess the church and piece of paper didn't mean much to him either." She took a sip of her wine then blew a stray strand of hair out of her eyes.

"I'm sorry to hear that. He was obviously crazy to give up a woman like you."

Her cheeks warmed at the compliment, and she took a sip of her wine to hide her embarrassment. "Thanks."

"I wouldn't say it if I didn't mean it. You said you have a daughter. How old is she?"

"Yes, Chloe." Her heart swelled at the mention of her pride and joy. "She's twenty now and studying history at university here in London."

"It must be nice to still have her close."

"It really is," she agreed.

The place was filling up with all the suited after-office workers popping in for that one drink before they went home. The clatter and general hubbub of the bar surrounded her like a warm hug.

Someone dropped a glass, and everyone cheered, and she and Guy joined in.

She discovered she was enjoying herself.

The time flew by, and when she had finished her glass of wine and he offered her a second, she accepted.

She found him surprisingly easy to talk to. He made her laugh, entertaining her with stories of his travels and things that had gone wrong—ordering items off a menu that he hadn't been able to read, to be served bowls of something that looked like it should be in a horror film. He told her about the time he'd accidentally taken the microphone from a Japanese karaoke bar home in the taxi, and how the bar's owners had chased the car down the street.

By the time she'd reached the bottom of her second glass, however, she decided it was probably time to go home. The alcohol had warmed her face and was making her all swimmy inside, but it also made her make bad decisions, and she didn't want to do that. She knew where three glasses would be heading, and since she'd only just met this man, she didn't want to go there. Plus, she always drank too fast when she was nervous, and Guy was only one third of the way into his second pint.

He indicated to her empty glass as a way of asking if she wanted another.

"I'd better go," she said, half standing. "I've got work tomorrow, and I can't afford to be hungover."

"As long as you're sure," he said, getting up as well out of politeness' sake.

She reached down to scoop up her handbag from where she'd placed it under the table. "I am, but it's been lovely meeting you, Guy. This went far better than I had anticipated."

"You didn't think it would go well?"

She arched an eyebrow. "Have you done much internet dating? The fact you're not a decade older than your profile picture was an excellent start."

"Fair point."

They stood, grinning at each other for a moment, and Neve felt her stomach flip. She couldn't remember the last time a man had had that effect on her, this immediate zing of attraction that she was positive came from both sides. She didn't think she was imagining it.

"How are you getting home?"

"Tube," she said. "No point in driving into central London."

"Agreed. Can I walk you to the Tube station?"

"Oh no, that's fine. I'm quite capable of walking myself."

Truthfully, she didn't want that awkward moment of him saying goodbye. She'd prefer just to leave him sitting here, so at least she was in control of the situation. She picked up her heavy winter coat from where she'd hung it over the back of her chair. It was still slightly damp from the rain. She tried not to grimace as she shrugged it over her shoulders.

"No problem. I'll finish my beer."

He got to his feet and leaned in to kiss her cheek. Was it her imagination, or did he linger a moment longer than he'd needed to?

"It really was lovely to meet you, Neve. I hope we can do this again soon. I mean that."

Her cheeks warmed. "Me, too."

She threw him one final smile over her shoulder and left the bar. The cold hit her like a slap to the face, though thankfully it had stopped raining. She huddled down into the collar of her coat and took a moment to get her bearings. She didn't know this particular road well. Did she need to go left or right to get to the Tube? She took out her phone to double-check, wishing she'd thought to do this in the warmth of the pub.

As she deliberated, she sensed the weight of someone's gaze lingering on her. She lifted her head from her phone, half expecting to find Guy standing there, but instead someone else drew her attention.

A woman was standing across the street, her arms wrapped around her body. She seemed to just be waiting for something, or perhaps someone, but it was already dark and hard to tell.

Why had this particular woman caught her eye? Was she watching Guy?

No, that was silly. She was just being paranoid.

The woman could be waiting for anyone.

NINE

Erica got home late.

She worried Poppy was going to become a latch-key kid now, and was mindful that she didn't spend too much time home alone. As always, Erica's sister, Natasha, had stepped up with childcare. The kids were at the same high school now, since they were in the same catchment area, and that made things easier. Natasha was there with Poppy to meet her at the door when Erica arrived back home.

Erica thanked her sister and then let Poppy into the house.

"How was school?" she asked.

Poppy threw her bag down in the entrance hall and kicked off her shoes. "Fine."

That was all Erica got before Poppy ran up the stairs. Moments later, Erica gritted her teeth at the slamming of the bedroom door.

She let out a sigh and shook her head. It was to be expected these days, what with Poppy being a preteen now.

She went to the kitchen and set about making them a simple dinner of pasta and a stir-in tomato and herb sauce. It was basic but fast, and it was something she knew Poppy would eat without complaint.

Sure enough, Poppy did, but the whole time she barely said a word, other than to give perfunctory one-word answers to the questions Erica asked her about her day. As soon as she'd finished eating and tidied up her plate, Poppy went straight back upstairs again.

"Don't you want to watch some television or something?" Erica called to her retreating back.

"I'm tired. I'm going to bed."

Erica stood with a tea towel clutched in her hands. "Oh, okay then."

But when she went upstairs half an hour later, to kiss Poppy goodnight, she found her daughter with the light still on, sitting on her bed, her skinny knees pulled into her chest.

"Are you going to tell me what's wrong?" Erica asked.

Poppy's young face was taut with misery, her lips pressed tight. "Nothing."

Erica sat on the edge of her bed. "It's not nothing. Come on, tell me what's wrong. Maybe I can help."

"You never help," Poppy threw back at her. "You only make things worse."

Erica tried not to flinch. She would allow herself to be Poppy's punching bag, if that's what her daughter needed. It didn't mean that it didn't hurt, though. Poppy had a life that was wholly external from the one she had at home. New friends, new teachers, a new miniature world all trapped within the four walls of high school. These were the things that were important to Poppy now; that someone said something about her behind her back, or she was teased for having the wrong bag or pencil case, or she was embarrassed because she didn't have enough money on her card to buy her lunch.

Erica took a breath. "I'm sorry. I'm doing my best, Pops. Things aren't always easy for me either, but no matter what happens, I'll always be here for you. You will always have me to come home to."

She wanted to be Poppy's place of safety. Her rock. Her harbour. But she knew after everything happened between her and Shawn, Poppy no longer felt like her mother was a safe place either. Though Erica was sure Poppy didn't mean to, it was clear she blamed her mother for losing the baby and driving Shawn away. For a while there, Poppy had been given a glimpse of the kind of family she'd never had—a present father figure and a much-wanted sibling—and then it had all been torn away again. Erica's heart broke more for Poppy than it ever had for herself.

Her daughter was growing up. Poppy was only a few inches shorter than Erica now. It was as if someone had put Poppy in a stretching machine, so she was all arms and legs. Her face had changed, too, losing that baby fat and becoming more angular.

Her room had also changed. The picture books had become novels, and the games were now body sprays and moisturisers. Posters of K-pop groups hung on the walls, and Poppy was more likely to be found watching random YouTubers than cartoons.

Now Erica had this new case to deal with, and she didn't want Poppy to feel she was even further down the pecking line than she already did.

How much more of her life would Erica give to her job? She was still a good few years away from collecting her pension, though she knew it would be worth hanging on for.

"Come on, kiddo. Time to go to sleep. You have to be up for school in the morning."

Poppy's eyes brightened a fraction. "Are you dropping me off?"

Erica's stomach twisted. "No, sorry. I have to be in the office early. I'm dropping you to your Auntie Tasha's house."

Poppy let out a huge sigh. "Sometimes I wonder why I even bother coming home at all."

"So we can see each other?" Erica suggested. "So you can sleep in your own bed? Wouldn't you rather be at home?"

"I guess," Poppy said, thumping her head into the pillow and turning away from her mother, towards the wall.

Erica leaned down and planted a kiss to the side of Poppy's head. "Night, love." Then she backed out of the room, switched off the light, and gently closed the door.

TEN

Erica hadn't slept well, tossing and turning all night. In fact, she could barely remember a time when she'd gone to bed and woken up feeling refreshed the next day. The last time had probably been when Shawn had still been living with her, she thought with a stab of pain that caught her breath. She quickly pushed the memory away. It wouldn't do anyone any good to dwell on things, and thinking about everything she'd lost made her want to crawl into a hole and never come out. She had too many people relying on her to do that—including the victim of this most recent crime.

She did that morning's roll call and made sure everyone had their actions for the day. The search for the gun that had been used was still ongoing, but nothing had been turned up in the local area. She was going to need to stop by her boss's office to see if he'd give authorisation to get the divers in. Her gut told her that the suspect would have tossed the weapon in the river, but if she was wrong, that was a whole lot of resources wasted. No one in their right mind would keep hold of a gun after it had been used in a shooting—not unless they *wanted* to get caught. If someone was found in possession of that gun, even the very best solicitor would struggle to argue their case.

About mid-morning, Lewis Crowe approached her desk. "Boss, Victoria Nestell's son is here to speak to you."

"Remind me of his name again?"

"Justin Nestell. He's in interview room three."

"Thanks, Lewis. I'll be there shortly."

Ten minutes later, she punched in the code for the interview room.

Justin Nestell was in his early thirties. He was blond, like his mother, but his hair was already thinning, making him appear older than his true age. He sat with his lips pinched and his nose in the air. His suit looked expensive. She imagined he was the type of man who would always speak down to the waitress at a restaurant.

Despite her misgivings, she forced herself to smile. She wanted to put him at ease. She wasn't sure if he had anything to do with the murder—he most likely didn't—but he would be able to give her some insight into Darren Blanton, or at least the kind of man he had taken Darren to be.

"Thank you for coming in, Mr Nestell. I'm sure you're busy."

He visibly swelled. "Well, yes, I am rather. I work in finance, so there's never a quiet day." He had the pompous, privileged attitude of a public school boy.

She gave a closed-lipped smile and took a seat. "Can I get you anything before we start? Coffee? Water?"

He grimaced. "I can't imagine the coffee is much good here."

"God, no. It's terrible."

He gave a small chuckle at that. "In which case, I'll pass."

She cleared her throat and checked the notes which she set on the table between them. "Good choice. How's your mother doing?"

He shrugged. "As expected. She keeps blaming herself. Says there must be something wrong with her for the men she loves to keep dying."

"How sad. She needs time to grieve."

"I guess, though I hope some other gold-digger doesn't see a vulnerable woman and decide to step into Darren's place."

Erica paused and angled her head. "You think that was the case with Darren? That he was a gold-digger?"

Hadn't she had a similar thought when she'd spoken to Victoria?

He twisted his lips. "I feel terrible for my mother, but I always knew that bloke was up to no good. What's some guy in his mid-forties wanting with a woman in her fifties?"

"Maybe he enjoyed her company, respected her. Loved her?"

Justin snorted. "Loved her money, more like. Loved that she put a roof over his head and handed him the keys to an expensive car."

"So you think he was just in it for the money?"

He threw up a hand. "Isn't that obvious? He wasn't a bad-looking bloke, kept himself fit and stuff. He could have been dating some thirty-year-old or even younger. What else would he want with my mum?" He shuddered. "Actually, I don't even want to think about it."

Erica gritted her teeth. He didn't seem to have much respect for his mother.

Justin hadn't finished. "They hadn't been together long before he moved in. I tried to warn her about him, but of course she didn't listen. She thought I was just being overprotective. The truth is, I don't think she's ever really got over my dad. She's been grieving for him all these years, and then that arsehole steps into his place. He even tried to do the friendly 'stepfather' thing with me, clapping me on the shoulder and calling me 'son'. He was only fifteen years older than me. Made my skin crawl every time I was around him."

It was clear that Justin had no love for Darren. How deep did that dislike go? Was it enough of a motive for murder? If so, would he really be so vocal about it, sitting here in a police interview room? Most people tended not to speak ill of the dead, but Justin had no such qualms. He seemed to be telling Erica exactly what he thought.

Erica hadn't had time to dig into Victoria Nestell's financial background, but she had sold a business, so she most likely had money. She knew the woman owned her own home in a decent area, and had got an impression of her not being badly off from the way the house was decorated and the vehicle on the driveway. First impressions could always be wrong, however. A car could be on expensive finance, as could furniture, and even if someone owned their own home, it didn't mean they didn't have debt.

She linked her fingers together on the table between them. "Was there a reason you thought Darren might need money? Did he ever mention having financial problems?"

Justin scoffed. "Not likely. He didn't mention much of anything. Oh, he could blather on about sports or the weather or what television shows he was watching until the cows came home, but if you tried to talk to him about something with any depth, he clammed right up. He never introduced my mum to any of his family or friends, and if you talked to him about work, he'd always say he was working on some investment or another but refused to give any details." He rubbed his fingers across his mouth. "When he met my mum, he gave her the impression he was some kind of property developer, but I ended up wondering if he was actually a drug dealer or something."

Erica lifted her eyebrows. "Did you see any proof of this? Do you know if he had any problems with drink or drugs?"

"No, it was just a gut feeling. Like, he got his money from somewhere, because when they first met, he was all about the wining and dining and buying her expensive jewellery, but then he was supposed to be buying a property, and the chain collapsed. He ended up with nowhere to live because he'd still needed to sell his place, and so Mum offered for him to stay with her while it was all sorted, and he never left."

Erica jotted down a note to look into the previous property the victim had apparently owned. Where had he been living before Victoria's place? She remembered thinking how victims of gun crime were often linked to gangs and drugs, and wondered if Justin's suspicions actually had some merit. Unless he was just using them to deflect attention from himself?

"This is all very useful, Mr Nestell. What was their relationship like, in general? Any sign of violence?"

His lips tightened, and a muscle in his jaw ticked. "Not at all. I'm not sure he ever even raised his voice to her. From what I could tell, he was literally a model boyfriend. He couldn't do enough for her. He was always jumping up to get her things and checking on her. As much as I hate to say it, I never saw my dad doing any of that stuff for her. It was always Mum running around after him."

"You're saying that he treated her really well, was friendly towards you, but yet you still didn't like him?"

He shrugged. "Call it intuition."

Or was it just that he didn't like the idea of a younger man finding his mother attractive? Erica wondered if his opinion would have been the same if it had been his father who'd moved in with a woman fifteen years his junior. Or would he have been patting his dad on the shoulder and congratulating him?

"Oh, one more thing before you go," she said. "You realise that being aware of a man being after your mother's money might give you a motive of your own?"

His eyebrows shot up his forehead, and he spluttered. "I hope you're not suggesting that I might have had something to do with his death. Do I look like the type of person who could murder someone?"

"Honestly, in my years working as a detective, those people come in all shapes and sizes. Please understand that I wouldn't be doing my job unless I asked."

"I was home all night."

"Alone?" she checked. "Or can someone vouch for your whereabouts?"

"I was alone. I live by myself. That doesn't make me a murderer." He thought of something. "But there is CCTV in my building. I'm sure it would have caught me arriving and would have caught me again if I'd left. I didn't go anywhere until I got the call from the police yesterday morning to tell me what had happened."

"That's fine. We'll be able to request the CCTV footage and verify what you told us. What time did you get home at?"

He palmed the nape of his neck. "I stayed late at the office, which isn't unusual. Then I grabbed a special fried rice from the Chinese down the road so I didn't have to cook. I think I got home just after eight."

"I'll need the name of the Chinese, too." She pushed the pad of paper towards him for him to write it down. She would get one of her team to verify his story.

"Of course." He jotted it down and pushed it back towards her. "Can't say I'm not offended by the insinuation, though."

She shrugged. "I'm afraid it's not my job to worry about offending people."

They finished up the interview, and she walked him out.

Was he right about Darren being up to no good? Not necessarily. Innocent people were killed all the time. There was a shooting a couple of months ago that was a drive-by where three people, including a child, were caught in the crossfire. None of those people had suspicious backgrounds.

Still, she couldn't ignore what he'd said. Would the property Darren had been selling at the time he'd met Victoria shed any light on his history? He didn't have any kind of criminal record, and most people involved in London's criminal underbelly had a rap sheet as long as her arm.

What secrets had Darren been hiding?

ELEVEN

Neve had been fighting off a lingering headache most of the morning. She used to be able to drink an entire bottle of wine in an evening and not feel it the next day, but now it seemed even two small glasses was pushing things. It was just another joyous part of getting older. Together with the painful joints and the way the fine lines around her lips seemed to be deepening by the day, aging wasn't a fun experience.

Still, her date last night had put an extra little boost in her step today. She was trying her best to concentrate on work, but she found her thoughts drifting towards Guy and the time they'd spent together.

Her phone buzzed, and she caught her breath, quickly snatching it up, hoping that he was contacting her to see her again. But it was her daughter's name onscreen, and she swiped to answer.

"Hello, love. Everything all right?"

"Yeah, fine," Chloe's voice came down the line. "I'm allowed to call my mum, aren't I?"

"Of course. I'm just as work, that's all." She tucked the phone between her shoulder and jaw and slipped into her office and closed the door so she wouldn't be overheard.

"That doesn't normally bother you. I can call back later, if you want?"

"No, no, it's fine. Honestly."

There was a pause, and then Chloe said, "Has something happened? You seem strange?"

Damn, how was her daughter so perceptive? She could hardly say that she'd been hoping Chloe's call had been from some random man she'd met last night, but at the same time, she wanted someone to confide in.

"I had a date last night," she confessed. "Someone I met on one of those dating apps."

She didn't want to say the name of the app—*Flirty After Forty*. It made her cringe every time she saw it, but then maybe she was just a prude. To her it sounded like the start of a cheesy television reality show on Channel Four.

Chloe squealed down the line. "Good for you, Mum. How did it go?"

"Actually, it was good. I'm seeing him again. At least, I think I am. He said he'd call. I mean, maybe he won't, but it was still a nice date. I enjoyed having a drink with an attractive man."

"Ooh, so he's attractive! Even better. And I'm sure he'll call. He'd be an idiot not to."

"We'll see..."

"So what does he do for work?" Chloe asked.

"Runs his own business, exporting china to far-off lands."

"Seriously?"

"Yeah, so he travels a lot. Singapore, Saudi Arabia, places like that."

"Maybe he'll take you with him someday," Chloe teased. "You could find yourself jet-setting around the world."

Neve giggled. "Don't be daft."

Even so, she couldn't help daydreaming. She'd only just met the bloke, but she'd rather enjoy a whole heap of all-expenses-paid trips to sunnier climes. Not that the possibility was what attracted her to Guy. He'd been good-looking and well-dressed, and there hadn't been any awkward silences. On previous dates, she'd found herself staring at the man across the table and trying desperately to think of something to say, but with Guy, the conversation had flowed. He had all his own hair, and had those sparkling blue eyes, too. He rather reminded her of that TV chef—the one who did all those baking shows, only a little taller.

"You deserve it," Chloe continued, "after the way Dad treated you. He was such a prick."

"Don't say that," she admonished.

"Mum, I'm twenty years old. I'm allowed to have an opinion on this, and that's my opinion. It doesn't mean I don't still love him, but I can see what a dick he was to you."

As much as she didn't want to hear her daughter speaking badly of her father, she couldn't help warming inside at her support. "Thanks, love."

Maybe it was time she had something good in her life. After all, other people met partners online and went on to have happy relationships. Why shouldn't it happen to her, too?

She was a good person. She let people who had less

shopping than her jump ahead in the queue for the super-market. She gave to charity. She always braked for small furry animals on the road. Being single had seemed to be a part of who she was now, though it had taken her a long time—years after he'd left her—to break from the sense that she was still married, even when her ex-husband had already been shacked up with someone else.

Now she felt ready to have a man back in her life again.

Her phone buzzed against her ear, and she lowered it briefly to check the notification. It was from Guy.

"Oh my God," she said to Chloe. "He just messaged me. I'm going to have to go so I can read what he says."

"Okay, but message me and let me know, okay?"

Neve agreed and ended the call.

She clicked on the notification.

<I was trying to play it cool and wait twenty-four hours before I messaged you again, but then I thought what was the point, so I'm jumping in and hoping that you enjoyed yourself as much as I did last night and would want to do it again. What are you doing this evening? Guy.>

She couldn't help the wide smile that stretched her face, and she fought against it, wrestling it back between her pressed-together lips. While she'd hoped to hear from him, she hadn't expected to see him again so soon. Was two nights in a row too much?

She stared down at the message and bit her lower lip. Did she want to see him again? From the way her stomach flipped and her pulse increased, she thought she did.

She typed a message back. *<I would love that. I did enjoy myself, too. When and where were you thinking?>*

<Same place, same time?> came the reply.

The headache all but forgotten, she typed. *<See you there.>*

TWELVE

DC Lewis approached Erica's desk.

"Boss, remember that security camera the owner couldn't remember the password for so they couldn't access the stored footage? Well, they were finally able to reset their password, and they sent us a copy. We got a hit."

"We caught the culprit on camera?" she asked, thinking that was a stroke of luck.

"Potential culprits," he said. "There are two of them. I've sent the footage over to your computer."

Erica twisted back around to face her screen. Her fingers flew over the keyboard as she pulled up the file Lewis had sent her.

"We know the shooting happened shortly after three-thirty a.m.," Lewis said, "but this footage is from before the shooting."

"How do we know it's the right people?" she asked.

"Honestly, we don't. Not one hundred percent. But watch the video. You have to admit, they're looking pretty shifty."

Erica hit play.

The footage was taken at night, but it had the night vision activated on it, so they were able to see what was going on. A ghostly image of the street in front of the house that the camera belonged to appeared in black and white. A couple of bugs flew across the camera, pale and ethereal. The vine of a plant located near the camera waved in and out of view with the breeze. It showed the small driveaway of the house and the Volvo sitting parked on the driveaway. Beyond that was the pavement with the dropped kerb to create the drive and, past that, was the empty road.

Erica's gaze was fixed on the screen, her breath trapped in her lungs as she waited to see the potential suspect or suspects for the first time.

At three twenty-eight, two figures passed across the driveway.

"Is that it?" She glanced up at Lewis.

He grimaced. "Yeah, I'm afraid so."

They'd barely been onscreen for a matter of one or two seconds. Erica rewound it and hit play again, and then paused it as soon as the two people appeared. They were both dressed head to toe in black, with hoodies pulled up to hide their faces. Their heads were down, so they didn't get so much as a glimpse of skin or hair colour to give them a clue as to who might be hidden beneath the material—not that it would have been easy to be sure of colour in the black-and-white image.

Neither were particularly big built, with one slightly taller than the other.

"Could these be the same teenagers who tried to break into Russel Whittle's house?" Erica wondered.

Lewis nodded slowly. "They certainly match his

description of what they were wearing, as much as he was able to give one."

She huffed out a breath. "But really, they could be anyone. With no actual eyewitnesses to the shooting, how do we know that these two were even connected to it? They might have just been passersby?"

"Even dressed how they are? With gloves on and their faces hidden?"

She made a face. "It's November. How many people *aren't* wearing gloves? And having their hoods up when it's close to freezing isn't unusual either."

Erica tried not to be annoyed at either herself, or Lewis, for getting her hopes up about the security footage.

"Let's get it to digital forensics," she said. "They might be able to increase the resolution and spot some detail that will help us narrow down who these people are."

"What about doing an appeal? Find out if anyone saw anything at that time?"

"Yes, that might be a route we'll need to go down." She thought of something else. "If these are our suspects, then we know what direction they came from. Why didn't they go back the same way? Say if they had a vehicle parked nearby, and then they needed to make a quick escape, why didn't they run back towards the car?"

"They didn't have a car," he suggested. "They were on foot."

"How far from? How far would they have walked? Does that mean they live in the local area? Or have they used public transport, and if so, which? The Tubes aren't running at that time of night, so did they get a night bus? Or perhaps they risked jumping in a cab or calling an Uber? Those are all things that will be worth following up on."

"I'll phone around local taxi companies and see if anyone had any pickups or drops-offs in the area that night."

"Good, and check the local night busses, too. I believe the N550 leaves Trafalgar Square and loops around the island before terminating at Canning Town."

Would the culprits have been stupid enough to use public transport? All the buses had CCTV installed in them, and using something like Uber would leave an electronic trail. If they'd jumped in a black cab and paid with cash, they might be harder to trace, but even some black cabs had cameras installed these days, though they weren't mandatory.

SHORTLY AFTER LUNCH, Erica got a call from Lucy Kim, the local pathologist.

"You got time to come down to the morgue?" she said. "I've got something interesting to share with you."

Erica pressed the phone to her ear. "I've always got time for something interesting. Be there within the hour."

"See you soon."

She ended the call and stood to gather her bag and coat. It was no warmer today than it had been the previous day. She wished she'd thought to bring a scarf with her this morning, but her mind had been elsewhere.

Before she had the chance to leave, Shawn caught her.

"Justin Nestell's movements checked out. I thought you'd want to know."

"Thanks, but that doesn't mean he's innocent. Could he have paid someone else to kill Darren?"

"He certainly seems to have enough dislike for the man, but then wouldn't most people in his situation? What son, or daughter, wouldn't have their nose put out of joint if it looked like someone was going to sweep in and steal their inheritance?"

"Maybe someone who wanted their parent to be happy with a new partner? It's not as though Victoria Nestell is old. She lost her husband when she was only in her late forties. Was she supposed to spend the rest of her life alone just to make her adult son feel better?"

Erica knew why she was taking this personally. She wasn't that much younger than Victoria and had also lost her husband. She couldn't help but empathise with the other woman. Was that going to be her future, too, to spend it eternally alone? Would Poppy be resentful of any man Erica might meet?

Not that she had much hope for her personal life. Perhaps being on her own was better? It was certainly less painful.

Sometimes her brain forgot that she and Shawn had broken up, and she found herself reaching for him, or expecting him to still be there when she woke up. Then it was like she experienced the loss all over again. She was grieving—the loss of the pregnancy and the relationship— but she preferred to bury herself in work rather than allow herself to feel the pain.

"Let's talk to Victoria's solicitor, see if she'd been asking any questions about changing her will," Erica said.

"I'll get onto that."

She hesitated and then said, "I'm about to head over to speak with Lucy Kim. She's got information from the post-mortem. Fancy a drive?"

He offered her a half-smile and a nod. "Yeah, I could do with getting out of the office."

THIRTEEN

They pulled into the car park, and Erica found an empty spot.

She turned off the engine and pinched the bridge of her nose, closing her eyes briefly. Her lack of sleep had given her a headache. It had started at her temples but had now spread behind her eyes.

"You okay?" Shawn asked from the passenger seat.

She winced. "Got anything for a headache?"

Across the central console, he bumped her shoulder with his. "Think I'm a walking pharmacy now?" There was humour in his tone.

"I'll take that as a no," she said, feeling the corners of her lips turning up.

"Sorry."

For a moment, she got a glimpse of the old them—how they'd always been together. It had been as though in those few seconds, they'd both forgotten what had happened between them.

"Don't worry," she said, "I'll nip in somewhere on the way back to the office."

They climbed out of the car. Erica huddled down into the collar of her coat, trying to keep the cold air off the back of her neck, and they hurried into the building. At the reception desk, they signed in and then walked the corridors down to the basement where the examination rooms were located.

She disliked this place almost as much as she disliked the hospital. It wasn't even the smell of death that bothered her the most—it was all the cleaning and chemical fluids that seemed to linger inside her nostrils. It made her headache worse. Death was something she couldn't escape in her job, and, instead of being hardened to it, she felt the longer she was in the role, the more it was bothering her.

Seeing violent crimes, and their victims, day in, day out...how was it possible for anyone to deal with it and not come out altered in some way? She wondered what kind of person she'd have been if she hadn't gone into this job. What if she'd become a florist or a baker? Would she be a different person now? Would she take things less seriously, and laugh more, and generally be happier?

The trouble was, she couldn't imagine herself doing any of those things. That life belonged to a different person entirely.

Her shoes squeaked on the flooring as she walked.

She glanced over at Shawn. His expression was unreadable, as it so often was these days. It was as though he'd built a wall around himself, and, most of the time, she struggled to dig so much as a chink in it. It saddened her that she'd lost him as a friend, as well as a romantic partner. It used to be that she'd tell him everything, but now all she got were one-word answers and him turning his back on her. He was never rude, always professional, but it still hurt.

She missed his family, too, and the raucous meals around the table cooked by his cousin's mother, Gloria, where she'd always felt welcomed wholeheartedly by the family.

Jasmin, Shawn's cousin, had spoken to her after the breakup and had told her how sad she was to hear about what had happened. Maybe as a woman, she could empathise a little more on what Erica had gone through and how conflicted she'd been about the baby.

They stopped outside the double doors that led onto the examination rooms. There was a buzzer to one side, and Erica pressed it to let Lucy Kim know they were there.

The tiny, doe-eyed woman with the crazy haircut and tattoos, that were currently hidden by her white protective outerwear, burst out through the doors in a flurry of energy that Erica currently wasn't feeling.

"Hi! Thanks for coming down here so fast." The pathologist chattered, seemingly unaware of the tension between them. "How are you both?"

"Fine," Shawn said, his smile tight.

The moment of lightness that had been between them in the car had vanished.

Lucy Kim shot Erica a glance, her eyebrows lifted. An easily recognizable expression of 'what's up with him?' Erica just gave her a small smile in response and a barely noticeable shrug. The last thing she was going to do was get into their history now.

"Good," Lucy continued. "I've got news. I mean, I've got news about your case, but I've got personal news, too."

She held up her left hand to display the ring on her finger. "I'm getting married."

"Oh, wow, that's amazing. Congrats. Is your...partner..." Erica didn't want to make assumptions, "anyone we know?"

"Yes, he's a doctor at the hospital. He works in ENT. Honestly, I didn't think marriage was ever something that was in the cards for me, but I guess he broke me down." She grinned to show she didn't mind at all. "You'll both have to come to the wedding. I'll make sure you get an invite."

"That would be great," she said, not looking at Shawn. She hoped the invite wasn't expecting them to come as a couple. "When are you having the wedding?"

"In the spring. We're hoping for a nice April, but I guess one thing we can never control in this country is the weather. It'll just be a relaxed affair. No unnecessary airs and graces. Just an 'I do' followed by a huge party."

"Sounds perfect."

"But obviously that isn't the reason I brought you down here. I've got something interesting about the case to share with you," Lucy said. "At least, that's assuming you don't already know."

"We won't know unless you tell us," Shawn said.

"That's right, so come in and I'll run you through it."

Erica and Shawn paused long enough to pull on protective outerwear and then pushed through the swinging doors. They followed Lucy Kim to one of the tables which contained the naked body of Darren Blanton.

Erica allowed her gaze to skim up and down it, automatically searching for any wounds—other than the obvious

Y-shape of the post-mortem surgery—that she hadn't been able to see upon finding the man's body at the crime scene. There was nothing that caught her eye—no additional bruises or cuts or even grazes that indicated a struggle. In the standard position he'd been placed, on his back with his arms either side, she couldn't even see the bullet wound.

Lucy came to a halt at the man's shoulder. "There are always procedures I go through before starting any post-mortem. They're important to ensure nothing is missed and no mistakes are made. The first thing I do is make sure I've got the right body. I always take fingerprints and DNA samples. That also helps me distinguish any samples I get that might belong to the perpetrator."

"Understood," Erica said, wondering where the young pathologist was going with this.

"Except, when I ran Darren Blanton's prints through the system, I got a hit on a different person."

Erica raised her eyebrows. "Are you sure? There hasn't been a mistake?"

"Nope. I ran them a couple of times, just to be certain. It seems Darren Blanton has a different alias. He's also known as Declan Starkey, and he was arrested and charged with grievous bodily harm eight years ago."

"Jesus Christ," Shawn said. "That changes things. Who was the victim?"

"Girlfriend at the time. A woman called Serena Jolley. She testified against him."

Erica turned to Shawn. "We're going to need to track down Serena Jolley and find out what she knows about Darren, aka, Declan."

There was nothing that required a person to notify the police if they changed their name, even if they had a criminal conviction. The only time it was necessary was if the criminal conviction was pending. To Erica, it didn't seem like a sensible way of doing things. They should know if someone with a criminal history was going under a different name.

"Could this be enough of a motive for someone to want to kill him?" Shawn wondered. "Taking revenge for something he'd done in the past? Perhaps he changed his name because someone was threatening or stalking him, and then they found him again, and this was the result?"

Erica nodded down at the body on the slab. "Of course, it still just could be the case that he was killed during a break-in and his history has nothing to do with this." The deeper she dug into the case, the more she felt it was unlikely, however. "From the people we've spoken to so far, there didn't seem to be any sign of domestic violence in their relationship. What did the neighbours say? Had they heard any fighting between the couple?"

"Several of them had known Vicki for years. They said she's reserved but friendly. Most of them remember her husband, too, and it looks like they were a little surprised that Darren moved in so quickly. But they said the couple were happy and they never heard any fighting or anything to worry about coming from the house."

Erica twisted her lips together. "Maybe it hadn't reached that stage yet. We definitely need to track down Serena Jolley and speak with her."

Shawn nodded. "Agreed."

This information opened a whole new line of enquiry.

She moved her attention back to Lucy Kim. "Is there anything else you can tell us that might be of use?"

"His blood alcohol levels are high enough that he'd have been just over the limit if he'd been driving. This fits in with the story that the couple shared a bottle of red wine before bed, though I guess he must have had more than his fair share. There aren't any narcotics or prescription drugs in his system, at least not that I've detected so far." Lucy stepped to bring herself in line with his hands. "No signs of any defensive wounds. I've taken scrapings from under his nails, but if he didn't get anywhere near the person who shot him, I'm not expecting to get much from the samples."

Erica had had the same thought at the crime scene.

"He had two broken bones that have long since healed. His clavicle, and the long, thin bone in his forearm, the ulna."

"Could they have been broken at the same time?" she asked. "In an accident, maybe?"

"It's certainly possible, yes."

Erica made a note of it.

"I retrieved the bullet from the wound," Lucy continued. "It was lodged between the C-two and C-three cervical vertebrae. As you already know, he was only shot the once. Cause of death is heart failure from blood loss."

Erica considered this. "So he lay on the floor, bleeding out? If he'd got medical attention sooner, would he have lived?"

The pathologist huffed out a breath. "That's difficult to say. It's possible, yes."

"The victim's partner hid upstairs. She was frightened the gunman was going to come for her next. I wonder if she'd come down sooner, or at least called nine-nine-nine, maybe he'd have lived."

"I guess that's something she's going to be beating herself up over for a long time to come."

Erica glanced over at Shawn. "We're going to need to

speak with Victoria Nestell again, too. She didn't mention that he'd lived under a different alias, but was that because she hadn't thought it was important at the time, or she'd been too distressed to consider it. Or, more likely, is it that she hadn't known?"

Shawn sucked air in over his teeth. "If he changed his name because he was convicted of assaulting a past partner, I can't imagine that was something he'd be too forthcoming with."

She remembered the interview she'd done with Victoria's son, Justin Nestell. He'd said that there hadn't been any sign of abuse, and that, as far as he'd been aware, Darren had acted like the perfect partner. Despite this, Justin hadn't liked the man. Erica was sure if Justin had any suspicions of there being violence, he'd have used it as a reason for his mother to leave, and she couldn't imagine he'd have allowed it to drop. But that didn't mean Victoria hadn't experienced it. People could look like they were completely happy on the surface, only for it to be a whole other story behind closed doors. If she was experiencing problems, her son would be the last person she'd confide in, considering he already had reservations about Darren.

Besides, not all abuse was physical. Emotional abuse could be just as bad. When someone is belittled and insulted and made to question their worth at every step, they became a shell of their former selves.

Victoria had seemed like an anxious person, but Erica had put that down to what she'd been through. She certainly hadn't seemed like a confident person capable of building a marketing company up to a point where it was worth selling.

Had Darren done that to her?

FOURTEEN

Erica insisted they stopped for coffee on the way back into the office. They got it to-go in paper cups, but it was still going to be better than the muck they got from the machine at the station.

When they were back in the office, she called everyone into the incident room to give them an update.

"We are working on new information that Darren Blanton was also known as Declan Starkey. He changed his name by deed poll eight years ago. Is this connected in any way to his death? Perhaps. Could this be a revenge killing?"

"Eight years is a long time," DC Howard said. "Why now?"

"Maybe someone only just found out where he is, or what name he's going under now," DC Crowe suggested.

Erica nodded. "Yes, that's possible. But I also don't want to lose sight of the possibility that this is just a break-in gone wrong. It's easy to be distracted by what seem to be more interesting answers when often it's the simplest one that is true." She looked around her team. "Does anyone else have any updates."

DC Lewis Crowe lifted his hand to speak as though they were back in school. "Yeah, I do. I've got Darren's bank records, and they make for interesting reading. Victoria was transferring large sums into his bank account on a regular basis."

"What do you mean by large sums?"

"Well, it starts off small—just a few hundred pounds —but within a couple of months of meeting him, it becomes thousands. See here, on the twenty-fourth of July, she transferred three thousand pounds. And again on the third of September, four thousand pounds. In total, from the start of the year, it amounts to almost fifteen thousand pounds."

So Victoria had been sending him money. Maybe Justin's instincts about Darren being a gold-digger had been correct?

"Didn't the son say something about Darren selling a property?" she remembered. "Is there any sign of that money?"

"Unless he's got company accounts under a different name that we haven't yet found, then no. There's definitely no deposits of the size that would indicate selling a property."

"This doesn't look good. Can you check into any possible bank accounts in the name of Declan Starkey, too?

Lewis nodded. "Will do, but here's the thing—there are other payments as well, for similar amounts, before he met Victoria. I don't think Victoria was the only person he was getting money from."

She was starting to build a profile of the kind of man

Darren...or Declan...had been, and none of it was good. "Can we track down the women who are on the other accounts that were sending him money?"

"We're working with the banks to get that information."

It was getting late in the day, and she was aware that she didn't want to keep everyone all evening again.

"Let's find out what we can about Declan Starkey—the man who Darren used to be—and then we'll speak to Victoria in the morning. We're also going to need to track down the woman from eight years ago, Serena Jolley, find out where she's living now. If she's not local, we'll need to send officers from that area to speak to her. Can someone pull the case file and read up on it, see if there's anything that mirrors this more recent case, too?"

"I can, boss," Jon offered.

"Thanks."

Erica wasn't even keen to get home, aware that it would probably just be another evening of getting the cold shoulder from her daughter. But she told herself that whatever Poppy was going through was harder on Poppy than it was on her. It was her job as her mother to be there, and she was keenly aware of how little time she spent at home anyway.

"We're still waiting on ballistics and a report from SOCO, but hopefully we'll have that by the morning. I assume there's no progress on the search for the gun either?"

Jon screwed up his nose. "Not yet."

She was going to need to get divers in. There was no point in putting it off any longer. It was already dark outside, due to the time of the year, but she could get them started at first light.

FIFTEEN

Neve got home close to eleven p.m., climbing out of the taxi onto the pavement outside her house. Her breath clouded on the cold air, and she shivered and tugged her coat tighter around her body.

It was later than she'd planned, but she didn't even care. She'd met Guy at the bar, they'd had one drink, and then he'd suggested dinner. He'd taken her to a little oriental fusion restaurant, and they'd spent the evening eating their way through the menu, drinking wine, and talking about everything and anything. He'd insisted on paying, too, not taking a penny off her.

When he put her in a black cab to take her home, he'd leaned in and kissed her lightly on the mouth, and she'd let him. She'd almost invited him into the taxi with her so they could see where the kiss would lead, but she'd held herself back. It was early days, and she didn't want to do something she'd regret. Besides, while they were both adults, she discovered that she cared what he thought of her. She didn't want this to be a one-night thing.

She thanked the driver and slammed the back door

shut. The black cab drove away. The house was in darkness, and her heart sank a little. There was something about coming back to a dark, empty house that made her soul heavy.

Neve let herself in and then wandered around, turning on lights and putting on the television so at least there was some background noise and the place didn't feel so utterly devoid of life. She didn't even plan on watching it. Instead, her thoughts kept drawing her back to that evening, and, in particular, the man she'd spent it with. She touched her fingers to her lips, remembering the kiss.

She felt like a teenager again.

She couldn't help holding herself back, though. In the back of her mind, she was constantly asking, 'What is wrong with this man?' There had to be something. That he'd never been married rang warning bells, but marriage wasn't for everyone. It wasn't as though *she* even wanted to get married again. Why couldn't she just accept that it was okay to have a nice time with an attractive man and it didn't have to lead anywhere?

It was self-preservation, she knew that deep down, and not only the kind of self-preservation that came from being careful about who you met on the internet. It was because when her ex-husband had announced that he was leaving her, it had come completely out of the blue. If he'd slapped her around the face, she couldn't have been more shocked. She'd thought they were just going through a bad patch. She'd never imagined he'd leave.

So she was protecting her heart as much as anything else.

Her phone rang, the number withheld. It was probably a spam call. She seemed to be getting more and more of them lately.

She answered it, "Yes?" Her tone was curt. She planned on telling them exactly what she thought of them calling at eleven o'clock at night, assuming there was even anyone on the end.

There was no reply. She tried to get a sense of some kind of automated system getting ready to play her a message, but there was none of that background hum that she expected.

Instead, she got the strange feeling there was someone else on the end of the line, someone listening to her as intently as she was listening to them.

"Hello?" she said, the hairs on the backs of her arms prickling. "Is anyone there?"

Still, she got no response.

She took the phone away from her ear and swiped to end the call. With the phone in her hand, she stared down at it. Could she block a withheld number? She didn't know why it had given her the heebie-jeebies.

Neve went to the window to draw the curtains shut. It was long dark outside. The naked trees, branches like skeletal fingers, were silhouetted by the glow of the street-lamps. A few lights were on in other houses across the road, and she imagined the lives of her neighbours, how their homes were still filled with the noise and bustle and laughter—and sometimes irritation—of having children at home. Or maybe it was just them and their partners, cuddled up on the sofa or even in bed. She didn't know of anyone else who lived alone.

Maybe she should get a lodger. She knew in this part of London, she could charge a pretty penny for renting out a room, especially if she included bills in the price. It would give her another beating heart in the home, someone she could pass casual conversation with over mealtimes, or maybe watch a television show with in the evening. But she didn't need the money, and truthfully, she didn't really want a stranger living in her home. Having some random person here wasn't the same as having family or someone she loved.

Movement from the other side of the street caught her eye. Was someone standing behind one of the parked cars? What were they doing there at this time of night? It was cold, too. There'd be a frost on the windows of the vehicles by morning.

Was the person looking up at her house?

The thought shot adrenaline through her veins, and she found herself darting behind the curtain so she wasn't seen. Had the person spotted her peeping out of the window at them?

Why would someone just be standing there? Maybe they were trying to break into the car?

Neve dared to edge her head past the curtain again, trying to spot if the figure was still there.

They were, and in exactly the same position.

Was it really a criminal trying the cars? Maybe checking the car door handles in the hope of finding one that had been left unlocked? If they spotted her, they might know she'd seen them and would be able to give a description to the police.

Not that Neve could tell the police much. It was dark and they had a hoodie pulled up to hide their face. They seemed to be of a slim build and not too tall, but it was hard to tell from this distance and angle.

For some reason, she was reminded of the woman who'd been hanging around on the other side of the street when she'd left the bar. She didn't think it was the same person, but there was something about them that reminded her of that moment.

But the person wasn't checking car handles. They were just standing in one spot. Not even hopping from foot to foot to keep warm or rubbing their hands together.

It was eerie.

Ghostly fingers trailed down her spine, and Neve shuddered.

Quickly, she yanked the thick curtains shut, closing off her view of the road. She exhaled a shaky breath. Why the hell was she so freaked out?

This was another part of living alone that Neve hated. There was no one she could laugh this off with, to diffuse the tension with before going to bed. Instead, she'd have to lie in the dark, worrying about the person who'd been watching her home.

SIXTEEN

Erica knocked lightly at DCI Gibbs' door.

"Come," he called.

She slipped inside to find him sitting behind his desk. "Morning, sir. There haven't been any developments with the Blanton murder case overnight, and our searches haven't turned up the murder weapon. Considering the proximity of the scene to the Thames, I think it's time we bring in the divers. I wanted to get your sign off on it."

He steepled his fingers at his chin. "Yes, that's fine. Do whatever you need to find the person responsible. You know I trust you."

"Thank you, sir."

She turned to leave, but his voice stopped her.

"I'm retiring next month, Erica. This is your last chance if you want to step up to DCI, otherwise you're going to find yourself with a new boss."

She hesitated. "I just can't, sir. It's not that I don't want to, but I'm already spending too much time at work, and I can't take on any more responsibility. It's not fair on my daughter."

"She's getting older now, though," he said. "You'll blink and then she'll be moving out, and you'll appreciate having your work then."

"But that's my whole point. I will blink and she'll be grown, and then I'll never get that time back. I'm trying my hardest to be present with her while she's still as small as she is, and if I take the job, I'll be doing the opposite. Anyway, by the time Poppy leaves home, I'll be looking to retire myself."

He flapped a hand at her. "Rubbish. You're still a spring chicken."

"A straggly old hen, more like."

He chuckled. "Very well. Do whatever you think is best."

"Thanks, sir."

She left his office and returned to her desk to put everything in motion to get the divers in to search the length of the Thames that was adjacent to the scene of the crime. She planned on getting herself down there as well, later in the day, though there wasn't much she could do to help. She wanted to see the area again, try to figure out if there was any area in particular that she wanted the divers to focus on. Would the flow of the river be strong enough to have moved the gun any great distance, assuming the weapon had even ended up in the water? Or was it heavy enough that it would just sink to the silty bottom and stay there?

The phone on her desk rang with an internal call, and she answered it. "DI Swift."

"Morning, Erica. It's Jasmin."

Jasmin had been working with digital forensics ever since she'd helped out on a previous case. Erica was pleased to hear her familiar voice.

"Hi. How are you?"

"Good," Jas said. "I'm good. How's things with you?"

"As well as can be expected," she said, not wanting to give too much away.

Jas knew everything that had happened between her and Shawn, and Erica understood that Jas would always take her cousin's side. Not that she even felt like there should be sides. What had happened between them hadn't been anyone's fault. Who was there to blame? Life was cruel, and they just hadn't been at the same places in their lives. It didn't mean they didn't still have love for each other.

"Anyway," Erica said, wanting to change the subject, "what have you got for me?"

"I thought you'd want to know that we've managed to get into the laptop that we took from the crime scene. It meant we were also able to access a dating site that Darren had been using. Darren Blanton was very active on there, talking to other women online, right up until the night he was killed."

"Talking?" she prompted.

"Yeah, but suggestive talking. Actually, some of it was pretty explicit."

"Damn. Poor Victoria."

The more she was learning about what kind of man Darren had been, the more she felt sorry for the other woman. Unless Victoria was hiding what she knew of him, it would seem that Darren was definitely not the perfect partner that he'd made himself out to be.

"Victoria?" Jasmin enquired.

"Yeah, his partner. She thought they had something special. The son was always suspicious of him, though.

Darren was younger than her, and her son always thought there was more to it."

"Do you think Victoria knew? Maybe she found out about his infidelity?"

"I'm just playing Devil's advocate, 'cause I know I'd be upset if I was Victoria, but is it infidelity if they were only talking online? We don't have any proof that he actually met with any of these people he was 'talking' to."

"It is in my eyes," Jas said resolutely. "If I found out something like that, I'd hand him his balls on a platter. Is there any chance Victoria shot him? Maybe she found out and killed him for it?"

Erica thought to the other woman, how she'd reminded Erica of a nervous animal. She'd been in shock and hadn't seemed like someone who'd be capable of shooting their partner at all. But women had snapped for less.

Still, the rest of the information they had didn't add up.

"Her hands were swabbed at the scene of the crime, and there was no sign of gunpowder residue on them, or on her clothes. If she been the one to pull the trigger, then we'd already know about it."

Jasmin made a humming sound down the line.

"What about the women he'd been talking to online?" Erica continued. "Any chance any of them figured out that he was already in a committed relationship?"

"Not that I'm aware of so far, but I'm still going through the messages."

"What's the app called?"

"Flirty After Forty."

Erica grimaced. "Yikes."

"Yeah, it's a dating site for old people."

"Forty is not old," Erica chastised her.

Jasmin laughed. "If you say so."

"Can you send me screenshots of all the profiles he's been in contact with? I have no idea if we can track these women down, but it's worth a shot."

"I can do that. I'll keep digging on my end, too, see if there's any more information I can find about the women. I'm still working on getting into his email, but there's also a possibility he moved some of the conversations off the site."

"Thanks, Jas."

They ended the call.

Erica scrubbed her hands over her face and sat back, letting out a long sigh. They were on day three now, and it seemed the deeper they dug into this case, the more questions came up.

She got to her feet and addressed the room. "Right, everyone, as well as taking money from Victoria, it would seem Darren was still talking to other women behind her back. We're going to need to try and identify and contact the women he's been talking to, if we can, find out if any of them know anything. Perhaps one of them is married or with a partner, and they found out. It would give them motive to kill Darren."

"Is there anything on his computer or phone records that shows he was meeting these women in real life?" Shawn asked from where he was sitting at his desk. "Any mention of days or times or places to meet?"

"No, but the messages get pretty explicit. I mean, if I was the partner of one of these women and I found those kinds of messages on their phone, I'm not sure it would matter to me that they hadn't met in real life. It's still cheating."

"Is it, though?" Jon Howard chipped in. "It's only words. Nothing actually happened."

"So you think sexting over messages isn't cheating?"

"Not really."

She arched her brow in disbelief. "So, if your girl-friend was messaging some other bloke like that, you'd be fine with it?"

"First of all, I don't have a girlfriend, but if I did, I guess I'd be okay with it, as long as it meant I was the one who got the benefit." He grinned, not needing to elaborate on what he meant by 'getting the benefit.'

"Well, I think most people wouldn't be happy about it."

"Enough to murder someone over it?"

"That's the question."

Lewis raised his hand in that way he tended to when he wanted to speak. "So who were the people in black caught on CCTV just before he was killed?"

"Maybe they had nothing to do with the shooting," Jon said. "They were just innocent passersby."

Erica pressed her lips together, considering this. Maybe that was the case, but her gut told her those people had been involved in the shooting. Yes, it was winter, but they were both dressed head to toe in black, and they'd had their heads down. Though they'd only been caught on camera for a matter of seconds, it was enough time to see they'd been moving with purpose. That hadn't been two friends getting home from the pub after a late night out. Their body language had been all wrong.

"How are we getting on with tracking down Serena Jolley?" she asked. "Anything on the old case file that throws up any questions?"

"Still working on it, boss," Jon said. "I didn't get much

time to work on it last night, and we haven't been in the office long."

"Well, let me know when you have something. I want to speak to Victoria again," she said, "find out what she knows. It's possible she has no idea what Darren has been doing behind her back."

"Do you think she'll admit to it, even if she did?" Shawn asked.

"I guess that's something we need to find out."

SEVENTEEN

"Ooh, who's the lucky person then?"

Neve looked up from her desk to find one of the security team standing at her office door, holding a huge bouquet of flowers. Two different types of pink roses made up most of the bouquet, interspersed with pink carnations and white calla lilies. It was beautiful, and the floral scent filled the room.

"Sorry?" she said.

"Well, I assume these are from an admirer? A local florist just dropped them off, and they have your name on them, so I thought I'd bring them up."

She got to her feet. "Oh, right."

"Must have cost a pretty penny, these ones. I wanted to get my wife a similar bunch for her birthday one day, and they were nearly eighty quid. I couldn't believe it. Eighty quid for some poxy flowers that'll be in the bin within a week. They must think we're made of money." He stepped farther into the room. "Shall I stick them on your desk?"

"Yes, I guess so. Thanks."

The security guard had left her office door wide open when he'd come in, and it was clear that most of the office had witnessed him carrying the flowers through to her. Plenty of heads were turned in her direction, craning to see what was going on.

She waited until he'd put them down and left, and then checked the small card that came with the flowers. She couldn't help but inhale their fragrance as she read.

'*Can't stop thinking about you. G.*'

They were from Guy.

She couldn't remember giving him the address of where she worked, but then she had said what she did, and she doubted it would be too hard to figure out which office she worked out of if he Googled her name. She was pretty sure it came up on her LinkedIn profile, or something like that.

"Ooh, are they from who I think?" Lacey's voice came from her open office door.

Neve's cheeks grew warm. "Yep. They're from Guy."

"He really is keen." The way she said it made it sound like that wasn't a positive thing.

Nasty Nigel came out of his office and spotted the flowers. He headed over, and Neve wanted to groan. Why did no one know how to close a door around here?

Nigel came to a halt in her open doorway, resting his arm up against the frame like he thought he was posing for an Instagram photo. "What's all this?" he said. "Someone's birthday, is it?"

"No," Lacey said. "Neve's got an admirer."

His eyes narrowed. "Neve! I hope you're not cheating on me."

Neve's blood ran cold. "I'm sorry?"

His face broke out in a grin, and he gave a small laugh,

but there was nothing funny about it. His eyes remained lifeless, and she had the sudden urge to turn and run away.

"Just a little joke."

She gave an awkward smile. "Right."

The two women stood there and stared at him, and eventually he got the message.

He cleared his throat. "Don't let this distract you from your work."

Neve wanted to punch the jumped-up prick in the balls. "Of course not."

He retired back to his office.

Neve and Lacey shared a look, both rolling their eyes and shaking their heads at their boss's awkwardness.

Neve loved the flowers, but she wished Guy hadn't sent them to her work. Maybe some women liked that sort of thing, with everyone making a fuss, but she hated the attention. She was a 'as little fuss as possible' kind of person.

The security guard had been right. This was an expensive bunch of flowers. It was all a bit crazy. They'd only met a few days ago. They'd barely even kissed properly yet. This was all moving way too fast. They needed to slow things down. But she didn't want to. Her stomach fizzed at the thought of seeing him again. All of a sudden, it was like her brain had grown incapable of thinking about anything else.

"He's love bombing you," Lacey said. "You need to watch out."

She laughed. "Watch out for a man who sends me flowers? Is that a new red flag I haven't heard about?"

"Is he paying for everything and moving really fast?"

"Is that not allowed now?" She couldn't help it.

Lacey's comments had made her defensive. She didn't want someone to step in and point out all the things that Guy was doing wrong. Not so long ago, it would have been commendable that he buy her dinner and flowers, and now it had turned him into an arsehole.

There was no winning this game.

"Things are moving fast, but he seems to feel the same way. Neither of us are exactly teenagers anymore."

They had seen each other every evening since he'd first made contact with her, and she was seeing him again tonight.

"Yes, but you're hardly on your deathbeds either. It wouldn't hurt to take a breath. I just don't want to see you get hurt."

"I'm a big girl, Lacey. I'll be fine. Honest."

She leaned in and inhaled the floral fragrance of the flowers, and a smile curled the corners of her lips.

EIGHTEEN

Erica decided to speak to Victoria Nestell herself.

She would combine the visit with swinging by the bank of the river where the Mets Dive Team were working and see if there was anything that might give her some insight into the case.

Her stomach knotted at the thought of how Victoria was going to take the news about the man she'd loved.

Erica was aware of how sensitive this subject was. It was never nice to hear negative things about someone who'd already died. It was cruel, in many ways. It robbed the surviving person of an opportunity to make peace with the news. They didn't have any closure, because the person was already dead. No screaming matches or fights, or tears or apologies. Just silence and emptiness.

She hated that she was doing this to Victoria, but what could she do? It was her job to ask these questions. Maybe she could have sent one of her DCs to do it instead, but she had Shawn with her, and besides, she wanted to see the look in Victoria's eyes when she heard the news.

Did she already know?

Victoria was back in her house now. Erica wondered how she felt, living alone in a big house where her partner was murdered. Did she lie awake at night, listening out for someone else trespassing onto the property? Every time she walked down the stairs, did she picture Darren lying at the bottom of them, bleeding out onto the tiles? Erica wasn't sure she'd be able to do it herself. She'd have wanted to stay with family, or maybe a friend, especially so soon after he'd been killed.

But perhaps Victoria didn't have anyone to stay with. The son hadn't exactly seemed like the most sympathetic of people, and maybe he hadn't wanted his mother to move in with him. He might have been worried that he wouldn't be able to get her to leave again. But Victoria was still young, and she was clearly independent, too, despite having Darren living there. She'd been on her own for several years before Darren had come on the scene.

They approached the door, and Erica rang the bell.

Victoria answered it, her gaze flicking anxiously between them. "Detectives, has there been any news?"

Erica knew what the other woman was asking her: had they found the person responsible for shooting Darren?

She shook her head. "Sorry, no. We do need to talk to you, though. Is it okay if we come in?"

Victoria nodded and backed away. "Of course."

She let them into the house and then closed the door behind them. "Come through to the kitchen. Do you want a cup of tea or coffee?"

"Coffee would be good, thanks." Erica did her best to make the other woman feel comfortable, and she always found that accepting a hot drink helped. It gave the person something to do and made them feel like they were talking to a friend instead of a couple of police officers.

"Coffee for me, too, thanks," Shawn said.

"I just boiled the kettle." Vicki went to the kitchen cupboards and brought out mugs and proceeded to spoon instant granules into them. In less than a minute, she was placing the mugs, together with milk and sugar, onto the kitchen table in front of them.

Erica noticed how Victoria's hands trembled when she set the items down. She was clearly still anxious about everything, and now Erica was about to drop another bombshell on her.

A part of Erica wondered how Victoria didn't see this coming, though. They hadn't been together long, and she'd already given Darren a lot of money. There must have been a part of her that had wondered if she was being scammed? In this day and age, how was it possible to *not* think that? Plus, she had her son in her ear, telling her what he thought of Darren, and, as it turned out, he'd been right.

Erica decided to lead with the money. "Vicki," she said gently, "while we were investigating Darren's case, we learned that you've been transferring large sums of money into his bank account."

She reached into her bag and pulled out the printout she had of the accounts, with each time money had been transferred highlighted in yellow, and slid them across the wooden table for her to see.

Victoria's throat mottled with colour. "No, no, you don't understand. I know how this looks, but I wasn't giving him money. It was a loan. He was a property investor. He had lots of different properties that he was flipping. But sometimes the bank would demand a payment before the house had sold, or a builder would insist on a down payment when Darren didn't have it. The money I sent him was an investment. I was going to get it back, plus interest."

"How can you be sure of that?"

"He showed me the properties. He didn't physically work on them himself, because he had teams of people to do that for him, and they were dotted all over the country."

"He took you to the properties?" she enquired.

Victoria's fingers twisted around each other on the table. "Well, no, because they were all too far away, but he showed me the details online."

"You didn't stop to question why someone who owned multiple properties might need to have investments of sometimes only a few hundred pounds?"

"Well, the money at the start was just to tide him over. It's not uncommon to be property rich but cash poor, especially if a sale has fallen through. It wasn't until later, after he'd moved in here, that he suggested me investing. It seemed like a good idea. The money would have made a lot more than it would have just sitting in the bank."

Even now, after he was dead, and she had two police officers trying to tell her that perhaps her partner hadn't been the person she'd believed him to be, Victoria was still trying to convince herself that she hadn't been scammed.

"Vicki, from our investigations, I'm afraid we haven't been able to find any properties registered in Darren's name."

"Well, they wouldn't have been. They'd have been bought in his company name."

"There's no record of Darren having owned a company either. It would have been easy enough to find under Companies House."

Her blue eyes turned glassy with tears. "What are you saying? That he ripped me off? That he lied to me?"

"I'm sorry," Erica said. "There's something else we've learned, too."

Victoria buried her face in her hands. "Oh God. What now?"

"Darren has been speaking to other women online. From his bank records, it would seem he'd also had other women sending him money in the past. We're still working to track them down so we can speak to them, too."

"No, I don't believe it."

"I'm sorry," Erica repeated. "You didn't know?"

"No, of course not. Do you think I'd have stood for it? I'd have thrown him out on his backside. When you say he'd been talking to women? When was this? Recently? How many? Were the messages...sexual in nature?"

"Yes, they were. I'm sorry."

"I'm such an idiot. What a stupid, stupid woman I am. I thought he loved me for me." Tears spilled down her cheeks. "I guess my son was right." Bitterness sharpened her tone. "I always was too old for him. He only wanted me for my money."

"Maybe money was at the start of it, but it doesn't mean he didn't still have feelings for you." Erica wanted to make her feel better, though she knew it was all but useless. "So you didn't have any idea that he was talking to other women? You're sure?"

"Yes, I'm sure. I would never have turned a blind eye."

Erica took a breath and braced herself. "I'm afraid there is one other thing."

"What now?" Poor Vicki looked as though she'd been battered by the world. Her shoulders were slumped, her neck bent, and she sniffed and swiped away at the tears on her cheeks with her palm.

"Were you aware that Darren went by another name? Declan Starkey. He changed it legally by deed poll eight years ago."

She shook her head. "No, but after hearing everything you've told me, it doesn't surprise me at all. Do you know why he changed his name?"

"We don't know if this is the reason, but prior to his name change, he was convicted of a crime. He committed grievous bodily harm on an ex-girlfriend and was charged with it."

Victoria clapped her hand over her mouth. "No! Are you sure?"

"Yes, we're sure."

"But Darren was never violent. Not once. He barely even raised his voice to me."

"I've got my team digging into the past case now, but I'm only passing on what I know so far. It does make us question whether he had a reason to change his name that resulted in him being killed. Maybe he was running away from something—someone else he took money from, perhaps? Did he ever seem worried or paranoid? Did you ever see him taking phone calls that he was cagey about? Or maybe he received letters that he didn't want you to see?"

Victoria thought for a moment but then shook her head. "No, not that I can think of anyway. Nothing that Darren did or said ever made me suspicious. He seemed like a happy, normal man." Her voice broke. "Honestly, I thought I had met the love of my life and that we'd grow old together. Now I know it was all a lie." She broke down in sobs, her shoulders hitching with every breath.

Erica exchanged a glance with Shawn. He grimaced, but he got to his feet and went to the kettle.

"I'll make you a cup of tea," he said, since she'd not made herself one when she'd offered them coffee.

"Shall I call your son?" Erica suggested. "Get him to come and sit with you?" She didn't feel right leaving Vicki alone like this.

"God no, he's the last one I want to see. He'll hold it over me. He'll make me believe I'm no longer capable of making my own decisions. Like I'm some kind of feeble old lady instead of a perfectly capable woman in her fifties. I don't want to hear 'I told you so' from him, though I know it's going to come eventually."

Erica didn't think her son was a very nice person. She hoped Poppy would be a little more sympathetic if Erica found herself in a similar situation in years to come. The thought made her shudder. Would she ever be vulnerable enough to have someone take advantage of her like that? She believed she was too hardened to ever fall for a con like the one Victoria had suffered, but then she bet most people felt that way.

Shawn finished making the tea and set it down on the table in front of Victoria.

"I'm sorry to have been the bearer of bad news," Erica said. "If you do think of anything that might help us, please, get in touch."

"Wait," Vicki said. "Before you go, who were the women? The other ones he was talking to? Were they people he knew in real life?"

"Not that we're aware of. We believe they're women he's met on dating apps."

"Goddamn him." More tears slipped down her face, and she blinked fast and turned her face away.

Erica and Shawn saw themselves out of the house.

"Well, that was uncomfortable," Shawn said. "Makes you wonder if Darren—Declan—got what he deserved."

NINETEEN

They left the car where it was parked outside Victoria Nestell's house and walked to where the streets became the pathway that ran alongside the river.

Unlike the previous days, today was bright and sunny. It was one of those late autumn days that made her feel like she actually enjoyed the colder months. There had been frost on her car windscreen first thing, and she'd even needed to wear sunglasses to drive to prevent her headache worsening from the glare.

Being near the water also made her appreciate the sunshine. While the Thames was its usual murky grey, the sunlight glinted prettily off the surface

Tourist boats dotted the river in the distance, but today this part of the Thames was dominated by the police dingeys that were protecting the area where the divers had gone in. They were focusing on the shallower parts, closest to the bank, but there was no saying how far the shooter might have thrown the weapon or if the current had picked up the gun and carried it deeper.

Uniformed police had created a cordon along the

bank, diverting all the joggers and dogwalkers away from the path.

Erica and Shawn showed the officer protecting the scene their IDs, and then they ducked beneath the cordon.

Erica recognised the sergeant coordinating the UCSST—The Underwater and Confined Space Search Team, better known as the Met's Dive Team. They were part of the Marine Policing Unit (MPU) but specialised as police divers. All UCSST officers were commercially endorsed divers and licensed search officers. As well as diving in waterways, they were trained to operate in confined spaces and hazardous environments.

This wasn't a job Erica would ever want to do. Maybe being a police diver might seem like an adventurous job role to some, she couldn't think of anything worse than spending all day submerged in freezing cold, murky water, grappling your way through all the silt and debris. Most of what they'd find would have nothing to do with the case either—random junk that people had tossed in the water because they were too careless to bother about disposing of it in a more socially responsible manner. Most of the time they had very little visibility. If someone was claustrophobic, this definitely wasn't a job for them.

More officers were on top of the surface than beneath —four officers for every one diver. The submerged officers were joined to the bank using a safety line.

Sergeant Dave Peake had been working as part of the team for twenty-plus years. He spotted Erica and Shawn over the shoulder of the fellow officer he'd been talking to and raised his hand in a greeting. He patted the other police officer on the shoulder and then walked over to meet them.

"DI Swift, DS Turner. How are you both?"

"Good," Erica replied. "Found anything of interest yet?"

"Well, depends what you'd consider interesting. We've found hypodermic needles, traffic cones, a couple of shopping trollies..."

"But no guns," she finished for him.

"Not yet, sorry."

The activity had drawn the attention of all the locals and tourists as well. Those passing on boats pointed and took videos and photographs, while those who lived locally peered out of the windows of their homes. The news of the shooting had been widely reported, so Erica doubted too many people didn't know the reason the police were searching the river. She was just happy it was only a gun, and not a body, they were looking for. That didn't mean they wouldn't necessarily find one, however. It had been known to happen before.

"It's still early days," Erica said.

Sergeant Peake glanced up at the blue sky. "At least it's not raining."

"Why, you're wet anyway," Shawn quipped.

"It's the visibility. It's shit anyway, but when it rains, it stirs up even more silt and brings visibility down to zero."

"Ah, I see." Shawn shared a glance with Erica, and she offered him a small smile to show him that she'd found it at least a little funny.

Sergeant Peake cleared his throat and turned his attention to Erica. "What makes you think the gun will be in the river? Is it just the proximity to the crime scene, or is there more to it?"

"Mainly the proximity," she said. "We didn't catch

anyone on CCTV running back towards the river. In fact, we didn't catch anyone at all after the shooting. But there are tons of paths and alleyways that lead onto the Thames. Someone could easily have cut through and tossed the weapon into the water, especially if they were on foot."

The sooner they found the gun, the more likely it would be that any prints on the weapon would be recoverable. The longer it was submerged, the less likely that would become. The divers had to scour every inch of the riverbed, mainly using their hands rather than their eyes to learn what they'd come across. It was a huge operation, hence the reason she'd waited a couple of days before implementing it. If they'd found the gun tossed in a bin or thrown behind some bushes, it would have saved all this hassle.

"I'm afraid this isn't a speedy process, Detective," Sergeant Peake said. "It's slow and methodical, and there's still no certainty that we'll find anything. There might not even be anything to find."

"It's been three days since the murder, and we're still no closer to finding out who did it, so I hope that isn't the case," Erica replied. "We'll leave you to get on with your work. Let me know the moment your team finds anything."

"Will do, Detective."

They went back to the car, leaving the river behind them.

TWENTY

They hadn't been back in the office for long when DC Crowe wanted to speak to Erica.

"Boss, I've found the most recent address for Serena Jolley, the woman who Declan Starkey—aka Darren Blanton—was convicted of assaulting eight years ago. She lives in a small village just outside of Reading."

Erica considered this. It was close enough that she felt she could justify the drive to speak to the woman face to face.

"Thanks. I'll be interested to see what she has to say about the man."

Half an hour later, she and Shawn were back in the car, heading along the M25 towards Reading.

"I meant to tell you," Shawn said from the passenger seat as she drove. "I spoke to Victoria Nestell's solicitor. She hasn't made any attempts to change her will recently. The last time was after she sold her company, and it was to ensure her son was the sole beneficiary."

Erica pursed her lips. "So, the only one who'd benefit from her death is her son."

"Could Justin have been worried that things would change if Darren stayed around for much longer?"

"Perhaps. Money is certainly a good motive for murder. If Justin thought he had some competition, it would be a reason to make sure Darren was taken out of the picture."

Shawn sat back and released a breath. "But why kill him? With what we know about Darren now, Justin could have hired a private investigator and destroyed their relationship that way."

Erica drummed her fingers on the steering wheel. "Maybe he did, and we just don't know about it. Maybe the violence in Darren's past was enough to make Justin think he'd be dangerous if he was simply warned off. Hopefully Serena Jolley will be able to give us some more insight into what kind of man he was back then."

"You don't think the GBH conviction is enough to tell us that?"

She considered this. "It helps, but it doesn't give us the full story. Is that the only reason he changed his name, or is there more to it?"

"We still could have sent some local officers to speak to Miss Jolley," he pressed. "Did we really need to make the drive ourselves?"

Her fingers tightened around the steering wheel. Was it just that he didn't appreciate being stuck in a car with her for over an hour?

"I made the call," she said sharply. "So yes, we did."

He turned his face to look out of the passenger window.

Erica let out a sigh and tried to focus on the road. They'd need to get onto the M4 shortly. They'd been lucky with traffic so far, but that could change at a moment's notice.

Soon enough, they were pulling up outside Serena Jolley's address. The house was modest but tidy.

Serena must have seen the car, as she already had the door open for them before they'd even climbed out. She was a small woman with light-brown hair cut in a bob and friendly blue eyes. At first glance, there was no indication she'd once been involved with a man who'd beaten her up.

"Serena Jolley?" Erica held up her ID for the woman to see.

"Yes, I've been expecting you. One of your colleagues phoned me earlier to explain. Said you were on your way. I'd like to say that I can't believe that arsehole is dead, but honestly, I'm not surprised he came to a sticky end. He got what he deserved eventually then." Even after all this time, her tone was laced with bitterness. "Sorry, maybe I shouldn't have said that, but honestly, it couldn't have happened to a nicer man. I'd like to shake the shooter's hand."

"Do you mind if we come in?" Erica asked.

"Not at all." She backed up, allowing the two detectives inside, and then headed down the hallway into the house. "Come through." She spoke over her shoulder. "Can I get you a tea? Or coffee?"

"Coffee would be great."

They settled around a kitchen table while Serena poured coffee granules and hot water into mugs, and then set them in front of them.

"So, tell me about Declan Starkey," Erica said, "or, as we know him, Darren Blanton."

Serena twisted the mug in her hand. "I wondered what had happened to the son of a bitch. It never occurred to me that he might have changed his name. I'd hoped he'd moved abroad or something."

"When did the two of you meet?"

She blew out a breath. "It was 2015. We met via a dating app, but things moved very quickly between us. He was the model boyfriend. From the first moment we met, he was always showering me with gifts and compliments. All my friends and family loved him. He was good-looking, and dressed well, and was funny and charming. All the things you could possibly want from a man. Honestly, I thought I'd met the love of my life and that we'd be together forever."

"When did that change?" Erica asked.

"After we'd been together about six months. He'd been stealing money from me, and I found out about it."

"What kind of money are we talking about?"

Serena grimaced. "Thousands of pounds."

"And you didn't notice?" Shawn asked.

"No." She shook her head and glanced down at her mug. "It was from a savings account, and I didn't have the app on my phone or anything. I logged in via my computer to make any transfers, and he must have watched me doing it and copied all my login details. I never checked the account that much, so a couple of months had gone by, and then when I logged in again, it was practically empty. He'd just been moving five hundred quid over to a separate account each time, so the amounts were never big enough to trigger any kind of alarm with the bank. When I confronted him about it, he at first tried to make out that he was entitled to the money since we'd been living together, and so all our finances should be shared. Of course, I wasn't falling for that. I told him I was going to the police, and he lost it. He punched me in the face and knocked me to the floor. Then he started kicking me. Honestly, I thought he was going to kill me. I think he must have thought I was dead, because then he just left. He left me bleeding on the floor, unconscious, and packed up his stuff and scarpered."

"I'm so sorry," Erica said.

The woman's face had grown taut at the recollection. "I had a shattered cheekbone. Multiple broken ribs. A broken nose. I spent ten days in hospital, and it took me months to really recover. That arsehole only spent four months behind bars, and that was awaiting the trial. The judge decided he'd done enough time, since it was his first offence, and let him walk."

"What about the money?" Shawn asked. "Wasn't he convicted for that as well?"

"There was no proof that he'd taken it. He claimed I'd made the transfers myself and the other account was a joint account, which he'd opened with me being unaware of it. Because he hadn't actually spent the money, no crime had been committed."

"I'm afraid we have to ask you these questions, but where were you in the early hours of Tuesday morning?" Erica asked.

"Here, at home. My husband can attest to that. I wasn't the person responsible for his death, though I wish I had been. I've beaten myself up every day, emotionally, for not fighting back. For not making him pay for what he did to me. Maybe now I can finally find some peace with it all."

"I'm sorry if we're making you relive your time with him, but it is still our job to find the person who killed him. We don't know the motives behind his death yet. It could simply be that he was in the wrong place at the wrong time. But either way, a dangerous person is still out there."

"Of course, I understand. You're only doing your jobs."

"When you and Darren—aka Declan—were together, did he ever give you any hint that he might be up to no good?"

"No, not once. That's why I let him move in with me so quickly. I thought 'why wait?' Or maybe he was the one who said that, and he just let me think it was my idea."

"Why did he move in so fast? Where was he living before?"

"He was renting, and the owner of the flat decided he wanted to sell. Declan told me that he wasn't ready to buy in the area yet, and that prices were crazy, and that there were twenty people all applying for the same rental property. He was at my place all the time anyway, so it just seemed silly for him to find somewhere new."

"Was this the house where he was living with you?"

She glanced around, as though reminding herself where she was. "Oh God, no. I moved out of that place as soon as I could. I didn't want to stay there with all those memories. Every time I looked at the kitchen floor, it took me right back to that moment of lying there, hearing the front door slam as he walked out, and believing he'd left me there to die." She took a shaky breath. "I do still believe that, by the way. I believe he'd left me there thinking I was either already dead or would be soon."

"You're married now," Erica asked, "and happy?"

"Yes, but it took me a long time to reach this point. I

struggled to trust anyone for a very long time. When I met my husband, I thought everything that came out of his mouth was a lie." She gave a small laugh. "Honestly, I'm surprised he stuck around, but then he's a true gem of a man."

Erica smiled. "I'm glad you found someone you could trust."

"Learning to trust again was the hardest part about what happened. It was as though the man I'd believed I'd fallen in love with and would be sharing a life with didn't actually exist. It was like a mask came off that day and revealed someone else completely different."

"I can see how that must have been hard for you."

"It really was."

"So when the two of you were together, there was no indication that he wasn't who he made himself out to be?" Erica doubled-checked.

Serena tucked a lock of hair behind her ear. "None whatsoever."

"And he never let on that he was in any kind of trouble? No strange phone calls or visits from anyone? No issues with drug or alcohol abuse, or gambling?"

One shoulder jerked up in a shrug. "If there was, he kept it well hidden from me. Like I said, I thought he was the perfect man...until he wasn't."

Erica had hoped they'd come away with some leads as to who Declan/Darren had been connected to in his past life, but it didn't look as though that was going to happen. Had there been other women who he'd screwed over in between living with Victoria and Serena Jolley? What had he been doing for the eight years in between? He'd spent one of them with Victoria, but what about the rest? Of course, there had been the time he'd spent locked up for beating up Serena, and then he'd changed his name.

Erica couldn't help but wonder if there were other women he'd mooched off of. Other women he may have even ripped off. Sometimes women—and even men—were too embarrassed to admit they'd been taken advantage of, so they wouldn't even report it to the police, especially if they'd willingly handed over money. They were hidden crimes.

"What about his family? Did you ever meet anyone? Friends, even?"

"No. He said they lived abroad. Spain, I think. I suggested we go and see them once, fly out there and make a holiday of it, and he'd shut me down immediately, said he didn't get on with them and it was the last way he'd wanted to spend a holiday."

He'd told the same story to Victoria.

Was it possible that it was the truth, and he actually did have family in Spain? Maybe they didn't share the same surname? It wouldn't be unlikely, considering he'd already had at least one name change, that they knew of.

"I don't suppose you remember where in Spain?"

She screwed up her face as she tried to recall. "I remember they were on the coast. Somewhere near Malaga, perhaps. I really can't be sure."

"That's okay. I appreciate you trying."

Erica hated to think of there being parents out there who didn't know about their son's death. Even if they were estranged, surely they still had the right to be informed? Or maybe they didn't care. They might know what kind of man their son had become and washed their hands of him completely. He could have even been their reason for leaving the country.

They thanked Serena for her time and returned to the car to make the drive back to London.

"Do you think there are other victims out there?" Shawn mused as she drove.

"Other women he's screwed over, you mean?"

"Exactly. There's a large gap between him changing his name and him moving in with Victoria. What was he doing all that time? You think he's the kind to have a steady job and keep his head down?"

"Probably not," she admitted. "You think his...activities...are the reason he ended up dead? That this isn't just a case of a break-in gone wrong."

Shawn shrugged. "You must be thinking the same or you wouldn't have gone to all the effort of meeting Serena Jolley in person."

"I don't believe in coincidences, and I don't think we can ignore the fact that this man clearly has a past."

By the time they got back to the office, it was getting late. She didn't know where the day had gone. Sometimes it was as though she blinked and hours had passed. She guessed it was a positive thing. She'd hate to be in a job where she was clock-watching the entire time and was desperate to go home. While there were parts of the job that were boring as hell—mainly all the paperwork—most days had plenty of variety to them, and she always needed to use her brain.

"Can I clock out now, boss?" DC Crowe called over to her as she approached her desk.

"Got somewhere you need to be?" she asked.

"Yeah, hot date." He grinned but then caught himself. "But if you need me to stay, I will. I can cancel."

"And have you miss your hot date? Not a chance. We've got it from here."

"As long as you're sure," he checked.

"I'm sure. Go. Have some fun for the rest of us." She needed to get home for Poppy, though she was frustrated by the lack of progress they'd made today when it came to finding out who'd murdered Darren Blanton, aka Declan Starkey.

TWENTY-ONE

Neve was excited to see Guy again, but also a little nervous. She needed to mention the flowers and how they hadn't gone down quite how he'd intended. Plus, Lacey's warnings about him love bombing her had left her with her stomach knotted in anxiety. She didn't want to think badly of him, but Lacey's words had struck home. Hadn't he been doing exactly what she'd described?

Neve didn't want to believe there was anything malicious in the way he was treating her. Why couldn't a man just treat a woman well without there being any kind of ill intent?

They met at a Bengali restaurant once Neve had got off work.

She noticed how Guy caught the attention of the waitresses, even though he was several decades older than them. There was something about the aura he projected—this self-assured confidence. It didn't come across as cocky either. He was always friendly and polite, no matter who he was talking to. She couldn't help thinking to herself that they made a good-looking couple. She allowed herself to daydream about the future. Maybe her daughter's prediction about Guy taking Neve off on holidays to far-flung locations would come true?

But no matter how much she wanted to think of the positive, Lacey's words still haunted her.

Was this all too good to be true?

"Everything okay?" He reached across the table to take her hand.

The air was redolent with the scent of spices, and quiet music played in the background. She hadn't eaten much that day, and her stomach gurgled with hunger.

"Sorry," she said, blinking, bringing herself back to the present. "Just daydreaming."

"You seem a bit quieter than normal."

She bit the inside of her lip, knowing she needed to bring up the flower incident. This was the perfect moment to slot it in, but she still had to force the words from her lips. She was worried she'd spoil things between them.

"Please don't send me flowers at work."

Hurt flickered across his face, and he let go of her hand and sat back. "I thought you'd like them."

"I did. I loved the flowers. It was more that I got them at work that's the issue. It doesn't make me look very professional and causes gossip among my colleagues. I don't really want people to know about my personal life."

He rubbed his fingers across his lips. "Shit, I'm sorry, Neve. I didn't even think of it."

She felt guilty for bringing it up, which was stupid. She should be allowed to set these kinds of boundaries. Even so, she had to stop herself from backtracking to try and make him feel better.

"It's okay. Just for future reference…you know."

"Sure."

An awkward silence settled between them, and she wished she hadn't said anything. She didn't want to spoil things when it had all been going so well. Trust her to mess it up.

Her gaze drifted across the restaurant, trying to find something of interest she could point out to restart the conversation.

With a jolt that sent adrenaline bursting through her veins, she locked on to a dark-haired woman sitting alone at a table near the back. The woman was eating, silver bowls of curry and rice set on the table in front of her. She sipped at sparkling water from a wine glass and had her head bent over her phone which was off to one side on the table.

Wasn't it the same woman she'd seen the other night outside the pub? They were in a completely different setting, yet every instinct in her body screamed that it was.

Neve leaned in to speak to Guy and lowered her voice. "Do you know the woman over there?"

He immediately went to turn around, and she had to grab his forearm to stop him being obvious.

"No, no, do it sneakily. Like, drop a fork or something."

He gave her a bemused smile but did as she said, accidentally knocking his jacket off the back of the chair so he could twist around and pick it up again. He took the opportunity to snatch a glimpse of the woman who'd caught Neve's eye.

He turned back around, lines between his eyebrows, and shook his head. "No, she doesn't look familiar. Why do you ask?"

"I'm sure I've seen her before. I thought she was outside the bar on the first night we met."

He shrugged. "Maybe she's local."

"Yeah, I guess so, though it's a bit of a coincidence that she's in the same place as us again."

"It's a free country. She must just have great taste in bars and restaurants."

He smiled at her, clearly trying to relieve the tension.

The woman obviously didn't mean anything to him, or he'd have had more of a reaction. Maybe it wasn't even the same woman. It had been dark that night, and she'd been across the other side of the street. How many dark-haired women in their forties were there in London? Probably hundreds of thousands. But it was less about her appearance, and more about the vibe she was giving off.

Still, Neve had already caused enough tension with the flower issue, so she didn't want to focus on the weird coincidence.

"So, when are you jetting off again?" she asked, thinking about how he'd told her on their first meeting that his need to travel often interfered with his relationships.

Maybe that was part of why everything felt so intense with him? He made the most of them being together because he knew he could be gone again for weeks at a time.

He took a sip of his beer, seeming to relax. "I'm not sure, actually. I've been able to do a lot more things from home recently. I guess it's one of the benefits of this day and age—meetings that used to be done face to face can now be done on Zoom."

That was good news, wasn't it? She'd worried that he'd be away too much for this to become something real.

"So true," she agreed.

Over his shoulder, she noticed the woman staring right at them. She wasn't eating, or sipping her drink, or even looking at her phone. She was just staring. Neve caught her eye and quickly glanced away, picking up her own drink to hide her discomfort. She was sure she wasn't imagining things.

A part of her wanted to get up and go over there, and demand to know what the woman found so interesting, but she also didn't want to make herself seem unhinged in front of Guy.

She did her best to move her thoughts into something else and focus on the conversation she was having with Guy, but her attention kept drawing back to the woman.

Guy was in the middle of a sentence that she wasn't paying attention to. "—and so I told him that—"

She interrupted. "Are you sure you don't know that woman? She keeps staring over here."

Neve didn't mention that she'd also been sure the woman had been standing on her street the other night, and she'd been staring up at Neve's house. What about the phone calls? There had been a couple of others since —all withheld numbers and the sense that someone was listening on the end of the line.

He glanced over his shoulder again and then twisted back around to face her. "No, I'm sorry, but I don't. I have no idea why she keeps looking over here. Maybe it's you who she recognises?"

"I definitely don't know her."

He arched his brow. "Would you like me to go over and ask her?"

She shrank in her seat. "God, no. It's just me being crazy. Forget I said anything."

Between her moaning about the flowers, and now fixating on some random woman, he was probably thinking that he'd made a mistake in asking her out again. Plenty of women would love to be in her place, and she was messing it up.

On the other side of the restaurant, the woman finished eating. She waved the waiter over, paid her bill, and then gathered her belongings and left.

Neve finally felt like she could breathe again. Why the hell was she so spooked? The woman hadn't done anything, other than look over here, and she could have multiple reasons for doing that. She might have simply been jealous of the seemingly happy couple sharing a dinner out when she'd been eating alone.

They finished their meal as well. Neve had drunk a couple of glasses of wine, and when he suggested that he came back to hers for a nightcap, she didn't refuse. Maybe it was because she felt guilty for almost ruining the date, or, more likely, it was that she didn't want to go home, alone, to an empty house once again.

They caught a taxi together, and then she invited him inside. She poured them both drinks, but they'd barely taken sips before they started kissing, and the kissing led to bed.

Guy was an attentive lover, and later, when she was left with a post-coital glow, she barely even noticed the missed calls from a withheld number that had been left on her phone.

TWENTY-TWO

Erica noticed DC Lewis Crowe had been absent from that morning's roll call.

He was sitting at his desk and had his phone clamped to his ear. Had he been on an important call and that's why he hadn't attended? Did it have something to do with the case? A breakthrough perhaps? But he didn't seem to be trying to get her attention to tell her something important. If anything, it was the opposite, and he sat slouched in his chair, his head down.

She bit down on a ripple of irritation. They were in the middle of a big case. She hoped it wasn't a personal call he was taking, especially as it meant he'd missed roll call. She approached his desk to get his attention.

"DC Cro—" She caught sight of her new constable, and her jaw dropped. "Christ, Lewis. What happened?"

He'd been keeping his head down to avoid anyone looking at him, but he must have realised he wouldn't have been able to hide his injuries for long. His lip was split, and his left eye was swollen with dark-purple bruising.

"I had one too many drinks and fell on the kerb."

"Come with me."

She took him into the incident room and closed the door. "Lewis, I have been a detective for more years than I want to count. Do you really think I'm going to believe that you fell over? Someone has clearly used their fist on your face. I think I can even see the shape of their knuckles in the bruises across your jaw."

Lewis was a handsome lad, with straight, fair hair and blue eyes. He didn't have a particularly big build, and was young-looking, even for his age. She could see him making an easy target.

He ducked his head, staring at the floor. "I fell," he insisted.

She sensed the shame coming off him in waves. "Did someone you know do this to you?"

"No!" he said immediately. "God, no." He exhaled a breath, giving in to her questions. "It was a couple of blokes who were hanging around the club I went to last night. I think they were waiting for someone they could attack. They saw me come out with someone, and I might have kissed him up against the wall." His cheeks flushed bright red, blending with his bruises. "But we both had an early start, and so we went our separate ways. Except I didn't get very far 'cause these two men followed me and decided to let me know what they thought of me, and people like me, with their fists."

"Was that all they did?" Erica asked him, studying his face. "They didn't assault you in any other way?"

She often felt that people with that kind of level of hatred for what another person did stemmed from something much deeper than simple bigotry. They hated them because they feared them.

She didn't think it possible for his blush to get any deeper, but it did.

"Definitely not. Seriously, they just roughed me up some. I'm fine."

"You don't seem fine." She studied his injuries. "Have you sought medical attention?"

"It's just some scrapes and bruises, that's all. It's not serious."

"There can be a psychological impact to being attacked like that, Lewis. You know that. Do you need to go home? Or speak to someone?"

"No. Really. I want to work."

"Okay, but stay at your desk today. I don't want you frightening any witnesses."

He tried to smile, but then winced as it hurt his lip.

Erica hesitated. It was clear he wanted to move past this, but she couldn't—not quite yet. "You know we should investigate, and find and charge the men who did this to you. If the bar has CCTV outside the doors, then there's a good chance they were caught on camera."

He shook his head. "No, I don't want to cause a fuss."

"These two men might do the same thing to someone else if you don't stop them. They might even go further. Once people get a taste for violence, it tends to spiral. What satisfied them at first won't anymore, and they'll get worse and worse. Did you tell them you were a police officer?"

"I don't think that would have helped," he said ruefully. "If anything, it probably would have made things worse. They seemed like the kind of people who would have reasons to hate the police."

"They assaulted a police officer," she said.

"They didn't know that."

"I still think you need to press charges."

He ducked his head. "Can I think about it?"

She couldn't force him, even though every part of her wanted to follow up on what had happened. "Okay," she relented.

She wasn't sure what there was to think about. Those two arseholes beat him up for the fun of it. She was furious on his behalf. Her mothering nature was rearing its head, and she felt like when she found out someone was picking on Poppy at school. It was the only time she had to hold herself back from wanting to tell a child exactly what she thought of them. Except this wasn't a child. These were grown men who'd made a sport out of attacking another man.

"I don't know if they would have even been caught on camera," Lewis said. "They made a pretty good effort to stay away from the front of the club and hide down an alley anyway."

"Our street CCTV might have caught them. It's worth investigating."

"You've got more important things going on."

"Nothing is more important than protecting my team," she said.

"Thanks, boss."

"Okay. If you start to feel tired or headachy, you might be concussed and you'll need to be checked out. Don't be a martyr."

Murmured whispers of gossip about what had happened to DC Crowe would quickly be going around the office. She hated gossip, but it was mostly unavoidable. The best thing to do was tackle it head-on and give everyone the information they needed, but that was up to Lewis, not her. While he wasn't hiding the fact he was gay from anyone, she also didn't think he'd want it announced, and definitely wouldn't want that he was beaten up because of it made public news. He was clearly ashamed about what had happened—even though it wasn't his fault—and she didn't want to do anything to make matters worse.

TWENTY-THREE

"How's Lewis?" Shawn asked her after she'd returned to her desk.

"Been roughed up. He wants to let it slide, but I don't think we should."

"Any chance he knows the identify of the person or persons who hurt him?"

She rocked her head back on her neck. "Damn. Why didn't I think of that?"

He arched his brow. "Do you think he knows them?"

"I'm not sure. I can't force him to name anyone if he doesn't want to."

"He's a police officer. He should know better."

"He's young. Cut him some slack."

Shawn nodded and then changed the subject. "I don't know if it's any use to us, but I looked into the app that Darren had been using to message other women—the same app that he met Victoria on. The head office is based here in London, in Shoreditch."

"Will we be able to get the information on the women he's been messaging? If we can get contact details for them, we might be able to speak to them directly. It's possible one of them knows something."

"Maybe one of them has a jealous partner who found out that they'd been messaging another man and tracked him down?" he suggested.

"It's certainly possible. The problem we have is that these app companies tend to be extremely protective about their users' data. Imagine using a dating app, believing you're anonymous, only to find that your details have been handed over to the police? I imagine it would be a PR disaster for the company."

Shawn folded his arms across his chest, the material of his shirt tightening around his shoulders. "I think they need to think about what their priorities are. One of their users has been murdered. Perhaps there's no connection between his use of the app and his death, but it's still a line of questioning we can't ignore. Hopefully, someone there will be of the same mindset."

"We already have the photographs and the usernames of the women from Darren's phone. We can work with what we have to track them down, but it would be helpful if we can get something more."

He nodded. "Let's hope whoever is in charge agrees."

THE HEAD OFFICE in Shoreditch was one of those places that was clearly designed with young people in mind. Cool artwork hung on the walls, and giant bean bags were strewn on the floor to create seating areas. No one wore a suit, and, instead, everyone dressed casually.

"Interesting how this is an app for the over-forties,

and yet everyone here looks twenty-eight," she said out of the corner of her mouth.

Shawn grinned at her. "That's because anyone older has no idea how the internet works."

Erica rolled her eyes. "Cliché."

He probably wasn't wrong, though. This generation had grown up with the internet. Doing things like programming had probably been taught at school. Whereas Erica hadn't even owned a mobile phone until she was about twenty.

Erica showed her ID to the young woman on the reception desk. She was barely out of her teens. The receptionist immediately seemed uneasy in the presence of the police, as so many people did, even if they'd done nothing wrong.

"Umm, our supervisor is in a meeting right now, but she should be out in about ten minutes. I can get her to speak to you then."

"We'd appreciate that, thanks."

"Okay, go and take a seat. Help yourself to drinks and snacks."

Erica and Shawn made their way over to the seating area, complete with giant bean bags and oversized games of Jenga. There was even a SodaStream to make drinks with, and a trolley containing snack-sized packets of crisps, nuts, and chocolate.

"Is this an office or a nursery," Shawn said, keeping his voice low.

"I have no idea, but if I sit on one of those bean bags, I'm never getting up again."

They snickered together like they were the kids.

A more smartly dressed woman approached, and Erica schooled her expression back into a serious one.

"Hi, I'm Anna Coots," the woman said. "I'm one of the supervisors here at Flirty After Forty. What can I do for you?"

Erica was pleased to see the woman in front of them was at least over the age of thirty. She might have even been closer to Erica's age, but she clearly took better care of herself. Her outfit perfected the 'casual but smart' style. Her makeup was perfect, and her jewellery were large statement pieces, but still tasteful.

"I'm DI Swift, and this is DS Turner." Erica cleared her throat. "This is actually a sensitive matter. Do you have an office we could speak in?"

Anna nodded and gestured to an area behind them. "Of course. Come this way. We tend to prefer more of an open-plan working environment, but we do have pods for those more private conversations."

They followed her to the farthest point of the office. The so-called pods had the interiors of grey, curved space-ships, clearly designed to be like modern art. Windows overlooked the London skyline, so they weren't completely claustrophobic. Like the pod itself, the chairs were also curved but resembled half-scooped eggshells.

They all took a seat, and Erica got started.

"In the early hours of Tuesday morning, one of the users of your app was shot in his home."

Anna's brown eyes widened, and she placed her fingers over her mouth. "My God, that's terrible news. I'm so sorry for him and his family."

"Thank you. I'm actually hoping you might be able to help us with our investigations, or at least point us in the right direction of someone who can."

"Whatever I can do to help."

Erica smiled. "Phew, I'm glad you said that. So, it

turns out that the victim was actually living with a woman he met via your app."

She placed her hand to her heart. "So lovely to hear about happy endings."

"Well, it wasn't that happy, considering he was shot and his partner found his body."

Anna blinked in rapid succession, her cheeks turning pink. "God, no, sorry. That was stupid of me to say. I just meant that we always love hearing that one of our matches led to a long-term relationship."

Erica kept the smile on her lips. "Of course, I knew what you meant. The problem is, during our investigations, we've learned that relationship wasn't as happy as it first appeared on the surface. It would seem at least one of the party continued to use the app long after they were already in the seemingly committed relationship."

Her expression pinched. "Oh, I'm sorry to hear that. Unfortunately, as I'm sure you understand, we're not in control of whether or not people decide to keep using the app, even if they've met someone through it. They're free to set up a new profile, if they so wish. We don't stand judge and jury over the choices people make."

"We weren't expecting you to. What we were hoping for, however, is to get the contact details of the user profiles he's been messaging. We have his username from his phone, and the photographs and usernames of the women he's been messaging. What we don't have are these women's real names or any contact details."

Lines appeared between Anna's perfectly shaped eyebrows. "I'm not sure I understand why you'd need them. Do you think these women might be connected to his murder?"

"We simply don't know right now, but it's an avenue we can't afford to ignore."

She gave a low whistle. "I'm sorry, but we really can't just give out those kinds of details."

"Even if it means putting a killer behind bars? I thought you were willing to do whatever you could to help?"

"Yes, but..." Anna glanced around anxiously. "Look, I've only been here a couple of years. I'm not even the boss. They're in China. This is just good marketing, having an office here in London. It makes the British users feel like they're on home turf and will have someone local to deal with, if they need to, when actually the majority of the business is run out of China."

"But you must be able to get your hands on more information. Even if it's just an email so we can contact them."

"I'd lose my job. I'm sorry. I really do wish you luck on finding the killer."

"We could use more than luck, Miss Coots. We will get a court order for you to release that information, if necessary." Erica knew the threat was an empty one. If most of the company was based in China, and was Chinese owned, things would get far more complicated than simply getting a court order.

"That's fine, if that's what you need to do. I certainly won't stand in your way." Anna checked her watch. "I'm sorry, but I really do have to get on now. I've got somewhere I need to be."

Anna got to her feet, and Erica and Shawn did, too.

"Right," Erica said. "We'll leave you to it, but you'll most likely hear from one of us again." She handed Anna her card. "If there is anything that comes to mind, I'd appreciate you giving me a call."

"Sure. Let me see you out."

They were clearly getting their marching orders.

"I'm sure we can find our own way," Erica said.

They left the office and went back to the car.

"I can't say I'm surprised that that went down how it did," Shawn said.

"No, me neither, but it was worth a try." She climbed behind the wheel. "I have an idea, but I'm not sure you're going to like it."

Shawn jumped in the passenger seat and yanked the door shut behind him. "What are you thinking?"

She twisted in her seat. "You're an attractive, single man of the right age. Why don't you set yourself up a profile on the app and then send a message to the same women Darren had been messaging?"

He arched his brow. "Sneaky, but you can't be serious?"

"I'm not saying you need to lead them on. Just explain who you are and what you're doing, and say you'd like to speak to them in person."

"They're not going to believe me. They'll think I'm some lunatic."

"Show them your ID. I'm sure they'll find you on the internet, too, if they search, maybe in some local news articles."

He huffed out a frustrated breath. "Do you really think that's going to make a difference? Male police officers don't exactly get a good rap these days, and male, black police officers will probably raise even more red flags."

He had a point. Besides, to do an operation like that, they'd need to get a trained undercover online officer.

"You're right. Forget I said anything." She turned the ignition key to start the car, and the engine grumbled to life around them. "I was just trying to think out of the box."

She didn't add that she was perfectly aware that her suggestion reeked of desperation. They didn't seem to be getting anywhere with this case.

TWENTY-FOUR

Neve had been buzzing all morning after her night with Guy.

He'd stayed over, and they'd had breakfast together. She couldn't remember the last time a man had made her a cup of tea in bed. That he hadn't made his excuses and run out as soon as they'd slept together last night had left her feeling more confident in the relationship.

It had been strange having someone else in bed with her, and she hadn't slept very well, but she didn't even care about that. Nothing was going to change her good mood today. Even Lacey had noticed, giving her a knowing look as soon as she'd spotted the smile on Neve's face.

She decided to take herself out for lunch. She wanted to treat herself today, even though she'd probably eaten out more this week than she probably should. Not that it mattered. Living alone, she found it was often the same sort of price to buy something while she was out than go to a supermarket and do a full shop, and then pay for the extra energy and time to make something herself.

She chose a little deli that did amazing toasted paninis, and opted for a mozzarella and pesto one, together with a latte. Even sitting there, waiting for her food, she felt like she couldn't stop grinning. Was it really obvious she'd got laid last night? It had been so long, she'd forgotten what it felt like. All those happy hormones whizzing through her system made her remember what she'd enjoyed so much about being intimate with someone.

The waitress brought over her coffee and panini. Both items were steaming hot, so Neve set them to one side to let them cool down.

The figure of a woman slid into the chair on the opposite side of the table.

Neve startled. "Can I help you?"

"I hope so."

Neve blinked at the woman. It was the same one who she'd seen in the restaurant the previous night. There had also been several missed calls from a withheld number on her phone when she'd woken this morning, but she'd been in too good a mood to give them much thought. Now, staring directly at her, everything slotted into place. The woman was also behind the calls.

"You've been following me, haven't you?" Neve said. "Why?"

"I need to talk to you."

"What about?"

The woman folded her forearms on the table and leaned forward slightly. "What kind of person are you, Neve?"

She sat back in her chair, trying to create more space between them. "What's that supposed to mean?"

"It means who are you, deep down? Are you someone

who cares about others? Or do you only think of yourself?"

Neve couldn't help her hackles rising. "Of course I think about others. I'm a mother, for God's sake."

"And what would you do to protect your child?"

She wondered where the hell all this was going. Was this woman trying to threaten Chloe? "Well, she's an adult now, but I'd still do anything. Absolutely anything."

"What about for a complete stranger?"

Neve hesitated. "I don't know...I've never been put in that position."

The woman lowered her voice. "What if I told you that you are in that position now?"

"I seriously have no idea what you're talking about."

"This man who you think you're dating—Guy—is a bad man, Neve. A really fucking bad man."

The woman slid a photograph of a pretty, dark-haired woman across the table. She appeared to be in her early forties, and was smiling happily into the camera, the ocean behind her, one hand on the railings.

"This is Lindsey. She's the sister of an acquaintance of mine, and she dated Guy. Well, I say dated, but what I should say is that he destroyed her. He took everything she had, not just financially but emotionally, too. She couldn't stand what he'd done to her any longer. Not only was she broke, but he'd broken her heart. She lost all trust in people because of what he did, and, two years ago, she took her own life."

Neve stared down at the photograph, blood rushing to her face. "My God, I'm so sorry."

Buzzing started in her ears; her heart was racing. Wasn't this sort of thing exactly what she'd been frightened of when it came to online dating? But she'd never imagined something so serious. She'd been thinking the person might be lying about their age, or might even be married. She'd never thought he might be responsible for someone killing themselves.

"Guy isn't the only one," the woman continued. "There are others like him out there, many others, and they all know each other, too. They have online forums where they discuss tips about what they should say to women in order to get the women to trust them. Different plays they might use. How to start slowly and work your way up, until they've taken the woman for everything they've got."

Her stomach knotted. "What are you saying? That Guy is some kind of conman?"

"His name's not Guy."

"It is," Neve insisted. "I'm not some naïve idiot. I've Googled him. I've gone back years and checked his history."

"It's not real, Neve. They put all these things in place. They set up different websites so they have a search history and make themselves appear genuine. They doctor dates on things, so you think you're looking at an old photograph when you're not. They play the long game so you truly believe that you're in a relationship with this person, and, in your mind, when they start asking for money because something terrible has happened, you're just supporting your partner, the person you love. My friend's sister wasn't a stupid person. If some random person on the internet had asked her for money, she'd have blocked them immediately. She never clicked links on messages or accepted phone calls that were apparently from the bank. She always called back a genuine number to check. But this bastard got her all the same."

"Didn't the people around her suspect anything?" Neve asked.

She still didn't know if she should believe what this woman was telling her. Why should she trust her when she'd been the one who'd been stalking Neve. She might be the con-person for all Neve knew.

"They didn't know. They knew that she'd met him on a dating app, and told her to be wary, but isn't that how everyone meets these days? And there have been plenty of happy relationships come from them. But not this one —except no one knew that until he left one day, and she had no idea where he'd gone. She even phoned around the police and hospitals in case something had happened to him, but the police just said he was a grown man and could do what he liked. As soon as she gave them some background on how they'd met, they just dismissed her."

Neve struggled to follow along. Her mind was spinning. "Even when she told them about the money?"

"She didn't. She hadn't told anyone at that point. She was brainwashed by him. Even after he'd left her, she still thought she'd been in a genuine relationship with him."

Neve felt her heart breaking for this poor woman. Was this really Guy they were talking about? She didn't want to believe it, but why would she lie?

"Bu-but surely after they did find out what had happened, they could have gone to the police? I mean, it's fraud, right?"

The woman's expression hardened with anger. "Do you think the police fucking care? They don't. My friend went to the police so many times after she found out that he'd taken her sister's money and then run, but the problem was that her sister wouldn't admit that she'd been scammed. She insisted that she'd given him the money voluntarily. But my friend knew she'd have never handed over all her money like that without being manipulated. It's happening all the time, everywhere, and the police don't do jack shit."

"What are you saying?"

"That women need to take care of women. We need to have each other's backs, and that means dealing with men like Guy—or whatever the fuck he's calling himself now—ourselves."

"Right..." Neve still wasn't sure what this woman was trying to get her to do. "I'm not sure what you want me to say? That I'll stop seeing him?"

She didn't even know if she wanted to promise to do that. Why should she believe this stranger over Guy? Didn't Guy at least deserve a chance to defend himself?

"More than that. I want you to say you're on our side."

Neve shook her head, still confused. "But he's never asked me for so much as a penny. In fact, he's the one who's always paying for our meals and drinks."

"That's part of how they work. Throw you off the scent."

Neve closed her eyes briefly and shook her head. "I don't know what to say to all this."

She'd completely lost her appetite, and her good mood from the previous night, and that morning, had vanished. She wished this woman had never tracked her down, and she'd never had to look into the smiling face of someone who was supposed to have been Guy's victim.

"Don't tell him that I've spoken to you, okay? Don't question him about all of this. You need to act as normal as possible so he doesn't get suspicious that you know."

Know? She still wasn't completely sure what it was she was supposed to know.

"Umm, okay, I guess."

"Good. Just think about what I've told you. Think about the lives he's ruined. Think about how, even if you choose to walk away from him, he'll just find another woman to destroy. You don't want that, do you, Neve?"

"No, of course not."

"Good." She inhaled through her nose and rose to her feet. "I'll be in touch, okay?"

The woman turned to leave, and a shot of panic went through Neve.

"Hang on, wait. I don't even know your name. I don't have your phone number. How will I get in touch with you?"

"You won't. I'll get in touch with you when it's safe."

When it's safe? How had she suddenly ended up in a world where she was no longer safe? Anxiety crawled like tiny fire ants under her skin.

The woman walked away, and the door of the coffee shop swung shut behind her.

Neve's coffee and panini had grown cold on the table. She was left feeling utterly baffled about the whole encounter. Was this woman telling her the truth? Now her stomach was twisting and churning, and she knew there was no way she could face eating her lunch. How was she going to be able to face Guy and not blurt out exactly what had just happened? She couldn't possibly have a normal conversation with him without constantly wanting to scream 'are you a conman?'

She desperately wanted to talk to someone about this, but who? She didn't want people to look at her and think how gullible she'd been to allow someone into her life who planned on ripping her off. Deep down, she'd always felt like those victims had brought it upon themselves somehow. That she would never have allowed something like that to happen to her, that she was smarter than that. But had those victims felt exactly the same way? It was like having your beliefs about the kind of person you are ripped away from under you.

Was this how it worked? The person made you feel so ashamed, that you isolated yourself from friends and family and didn't tell them what was going on? Wasn't that what the woman said her friend's sister had done?

But this was different. Neve hadn't given Guy anything. They were just seeing each other, and the worst part was that she liked him. She liked him more than she had liked any man since she'd met her ex-husband. She had no proof that the things this woman accused him of were real. She hadn't even got the full name of the sister so she could research her death. The woman had basically stalked her for the past week, and now she was supposed to just take everything at face value? Why should she trust that stranger's word any more or less than she should trust Guy's?

She buried her face in her hands. She wanted to go home, lock the door, put her phone on 'do not disturb', and hide away in bed.

"Is everything okay with your meal?"

The waitress's voice beside her made her jump.

"I'm sorry," Neve said, getting to her feet. "I've had a family emergency. I have to leave."

"I can get those packaged up to take with you," the waitress offered.

Neve rummaged around in her handbag for her purse, located a ten-pound note, and slid it onto the table.

"No, that won't be necessary, but thank you."

Keeping her head down, she hurried from the café

and exited into the crisp air. She checked up and down the street for any sign of the woman, but she was nowhere to be seen.

Had that encounter really just happened? She didn't know what to think. How was she supposed to go back to work now and focus on her job? She had far too many questions. The first thing she wanted to do was jump online and search him up again, try to spot cracks in the story she'd been told.

Her heart sank as she remembered she was supposed to be meeting Guy for dinner. She checked her watch. That was only four hours from now. Should she cancel? She'd been looking forward to seeing him, but now she wasn't sure. He'd notice something was wrong, and then what would she say?

But the woman had told her to just act normally, to not give any indication to Guy that she might know more.

Neve wasn't sure she was that good of an actress, but maybe she was going to have to try.

TWENTY-FIVE

Erica grabbed a quick lunch from the sandwich shop around the corner. As she walked back in, from across the office, DC Jon Howard lifted his hand to get her attention.

"I've got something you'd probably like to see," he said as she went over. "I've been digging into the case involving Russel Whittle and the baseball bat."

"Oh, yes? What have you found?"

"I followed the route that Mr Whittle said the youths had been heading and checked out what CCTV I could find from that area at that time, and I got a hit."

"That's great news."

Jon nodded. "We picked up their faces on street cameras just past the big supermarket about ten minutes after Mr Whittle says he chased them in that direction."

She grabbed a chair and perched on the edge, eager to see the footage. "How do we know it's the same people?"

"Well, we don't, not completely, but look." He hit play on the street CCTV footage. "They're all dressed in black, and there seems to be something hanging out of one of their pockets."

The people onscreen were all young men—late teens or early twenties. Despite having just been chased by a six-feet-something bearded man with a baseball bat, they didn't seem overly worried. They laughed together, bumping each other's shoulders as they walked.

What time had the CCTV footage been taken? Did it fit in with Mr Whittle's police report? Erica checked the corner of the screen. Yes, it did.

"A hat," she said, focusing in on the item hanging from one of their pockets. "A black woollen hat."

"Or a balaclava?" he suggested. "But that's not even the best part. I got digital forensics to run facial recognition software on the images we were able to grab, and we got a hit. One of the men is known to us. His name is Cole Seger. He's only twenty years old, but he's already served time. He's already been charged with domestic burglary, theft, and for shoplifting. Honestly, I'm only surprised we didn't find him behind bars right now."

"He's a professional thief," she said.

"Well, he'd be more professional if he wasn't getting caught all the time, but yes, he does seem to have made a very poor career of it. In none of the cases, however, was he ever found with a weapon, so it's a pretty big jump up from where he was to suddenly start carrying a gun."

Erica considered this. "Perhaps he had a reason to. Someone threatening him, maybe? Do we have a recent address for him?"

"Yes, and he's local. Looks like he's still living at home with his mother."

"What about the people he was with?"

"Not sure yet. We didn't get a hit on them. Their faces weren't direct or clear enough."

"Okay, well, let's bring him in. Find out where he was the night of the shooting. See what he knows." She paused and pursed her lips. "Who was investigating the Whittle case anyway? Why didn't they get this footage the first time around? It's lazy police work. If he is the one responsible for Darren's death, they could have prevented a murder."

The investigating officers clearly hadn't taken Mr Whittle seriously. Had it been because of his appearance, or because he lived in ex-council housing? She was fully aware that there was prejudice in the force, and that prejudice took form in all shapes and sizes—religion, skin colour, sex, wealth. It was all alive and kicking.

It wasn't her job to tell another officer that they weren't doing their job correctly. Resources were strained, and perhaps they didn't have enough manpower to investigate an alleged break-in. Maybe they had their reasons for letting this slide.

A COUPLE OF HOURS LATER, she got the call that Cole Seger had been located and brought in for questioning. Now she stood outside interview room two, staring through the window at the sullen youth sitting on the other side of the table.

Was she looking at the person responsible for shooting Darren Blanton? Cole Seger was a serial offender. He'd started as a young teen, shoplifting, which had then developed into theft—pick pocketing and pinching handbags—until he'd grown bored of that and turned to domestic burglary. He'd never been violent, though. Had never even been found with a knife on him, which was unusual in this day and age. Was it really possible that he'd have carried a gun to break into Victoria Nestell's house?

The severity of crimes did tend to increase the longer the perpetrator had been carrying them out. Perhaps in this case, his crimes had escalated to murder?

She entered the room. "Mr Seger? My name is DI Swift. I was hoping to ask you a few questions."

The young man shrugged. "Not like I've got much choice, do I?"

"Do you understand why you're here?"

"Nope. I haven't done nothing."

"You're here under suspicion of an attempted breaking and entering of a property on the fourteen of November." She read him his rights, and then added, "You can call a solicitor, or we can provide one."

"No bother. They're a waste of time. Never done me any good before."

"Can I get you anything before we start? Water? Coffee? Tea?"

He shook his head. "Nah. I don't need anything. I'm not planning on being here that long."

Erica refrained from telling him that it wasn't exactly his choice.

"Right, I'll get started then." She reached into her bag and pulled out the still images that had been taken from the CCTV cameras. "In the early hours of November fourteenth, a local resident claims you were trying to break into his house. He stopped you with a baseball bat, and you ran away, in the direction these images were taken only a matter of minutes later. Does any of this sound familiar?"

"Yeah, it does, but I didn't even do nothing! We were just walking along the street, minding our own business, and this fucking nutter comes running out of the house with a baseball bat!"

"You ran away," Erica pointed out, as though that somehow confirmed his guilt.

"What the hell else was I supposed to do? You'd run away if he was chasing you in the middle of the night, too. Have you seen the size of him? Plus, he had the fucking bat. I should have been the one who reported him, not the other way around."

"He says you were trying to break into his house."

"Bullshit. We were just hanging. Maybe we were being a bit loud, but that's all. We weren't doing anything wrong."

"Your priors would argue otherwise."

He sniffed and jerked one shoulder. "Yeah, but I was just a kid then. I'm twenty now. I'm making some changes. Doing some good in my life."

"Is that so?"

"Yeah, it fucking is, all right."

"What about the other two you were with?" she asked. "What would they say if we asked them?"

"Same as what I've said."

"Can you give me their names."

He stared at her for a moment and then laughed. "So you don't know who they are?"

She allowed the corners of her lips to lift. "I was hoping you'd help with that."

"And why the fuck would I do that? I'm not helping no cops. Do you think I'm a grass?"

Erica held in a sigh and regrouped her thoughts. "You said you were making some changes. Do those changes involve carrying a gun to your next break-in so you'd be better armed in case you came across a man with a baseball bat?"

"What?" He clucked his tongue against the roof of his mouth. "Nah, man. No way. I don't deal with shit like that. I'm not going down again, especially not for something like that. I told you already, I'm cleaning up my act. That bloke with the bat was the nut job."

"Where were you in the early hours of Tuesday morning?"

"What's this got to do with that break-in? You've got me in here on false pretences, haven't you, Detective? It's not really the attempted break-in you're worried about. It's the shooting." Worry crossed his features for the first time. "I didn't have anything to do with that. You need to let me go."

She gritted her teeth. "A man is dead, Cole, and finding out who killed him is at the top of my priorities."

"Why the fuck are you wasting your time in here, speaking to me then?"

"Because part of the investigation is ruling people out, and if there's no possibility that either you or your friends were responsible for the shooting, then I'd like to be able to cross you off the list. But if you won't talk to me, then you make that impossible, and I have to keep wasting both our time."

Cole crossed his arms over his chest and pressed his lips into a thin line. He turned his face away from her, and she could see he was considering what she'd said. Did that mean he wasn't the person responsible for shooting

Darren Blanton? But that didn't mean he didn't know who was responsible. Sometimes whispers went around the housing estates, telling of the gossip about who did what.

Erica remained silent, allowing the young man's mind to do the work for her. Silence could be a good way of getting someone to talk. They felt the need to fill it. But Cole remained stubbornly silent.

She tried again. "Where were you when the shooting happened, Cole?"

"At home, in bed."

"Is there anyone who can confirm that?"

His lips pinched. "Yeah, my mum."

Erica was sure his mother would say whatever was needed to protect her son. Even if she did believe he'd been home that night, could she really be certain? How easy would it have been for him to slip out after he'd arrived home? After all, Cole was an adult, despite still living with his mother. He could easily have sneaked down the stairs and left the property without his parent's knowledge.

"Do you know this man? Darren Blanton?" She slid a photograph of the victim across the table.

He scoffed. "No. Why the hell would I?"

"You might have known him in a different name? Declan Starkey."

"No. I already told you, I don't know him." He was starting to get agitated.

"Look, Cole. You and I want the same thing here."

He arched an eyebrow. "We do?"

"I want to be able to rule you out of the investigation so you can walk out of here, and you want to be able to leave. So why don't we save both of us a lot of time and just be straight with one another. Who were the other two men you were with?"

She pushed a printout of a screen image from the CCTV and tapped the picture with her nail.

"I don't know them. They were just walking with me."

"Sure. You just walk down the street in the middle of two random men you don't know?"

He shrugged. "They were being friendly."

"At that time in the morning?"

"You can be friendly at any time, Detective."

This could all be a complete waste of time. They didn't even have any proof that Cole was connected to the shooting, only that he was involved in a suspected break-in attempt close by a few weeks earlier.

She showed him a second printout—this one of the two people in black who'd walked past the neighbour's CCTV camera shortly before the shooting.

"Is one of these people you?"

From the size and shape, it could have been.

"No! This is bullshit," Cole said, throwing up his hands. "You don't have anything to charge me with, do you? If you can't charge me, you need to let me go."

He was right, she didn't. Suspected breaking and entering? He didn't even do that. The prisons were full right now. They were even releasing men who'd actually been convicted of crimes and given a sentence because they simply didn't have anywhere to put them. While she wished men like Cole weren't wandering the streets, the CPS would laugh her out of the room if she brought this to them. All they had was one man's word against the other, and both of them had criminal convictions already.

Plus, she had no proof whatsoever that he was linked to the shooting. It was all just circumstantial.

"Very well, Cole. I'll get one of my officers to see you out. Thank you for your time."

She gathered her paperwork and slid it back into her bag and then left the room. She knew Shawn had been watching the interview remotely, so she went to join him in the office.

"What do you think?" she asked him.

"He was definitely one of the people who Mr Whittle chased with a bat, but do I think he also killed Darren Blanton? No, I don't."

She agreed. "He seemed genuinely shocked and worried when I brought it up."

"Kid could just be an excellent actor."

"True. I mean, it's not as though we haven't come across very good liars before. He'd want to protect himself." Erica considered their next steps. "Let's see if we can pin down where he was the night of the shooting for sure. Check the alibi with his mother. Does he drive? If he has a car, or maybe if his mother has a car, see if it was in the local area at that time. Check for any CCTV around his home where we might have caught him leaving or coming home during the hours either side of the murder. I guess this is a case of ruling him out as much as ruling him in."

"Got it," Shawn said.

A crime was a puzzle, but sometimes it felt as though the deeper she dug, she only discovered more questions instead of answers. She was being led down two very separate streets. The first was that Darren was simply in the wrong place at the wrong time. The second was that someone had a reason for wanting him dead. She couldn't ignore either path.

TWENTY-SIX

Erica finally finished work and went to pick up her daughter.

Natasha took her to one side and lowered her voice so the kids didn't overhear. "We've had a bit of drama here. Poppy's broken her phone. It happened at school."

"What? She's normally so careful."

"The screen is shattered."

Erica tried not to be disappointed. "How the hell did she manage that?"

"She says she doesn't know. That it was in her pocket and she just found it like that." Natasha bit her lower lip, worrying at a piece of skin. "But I don't know, something just seems off."

"You think there's more to the story? What do her cousins say?"

"That there are some mean girls at school who were laughing at Poppy behind her back. They're the popular girls, you know the type."

"Do they think these girls had something to do with Poppy's broken phone?"

Natasha shrugged. "It's impossible to know for sure from gossip, but I've just got a feeling."

"Did her cousins say anything to these girls? Stick up for Poppy?"

"I don't think so. It's normally best not to escalate these things by getting other kids involved."

Erica released a breath and scrubbed her hand across her eyes. "Yeah, of course. Shit. I'm going to need to talk to the school again. Can they at least keep an eye out for her when she's there?"

"They do, I'm sure, but they're in different years so it's not always easy."

Erica hated to think of poor Poppy floating around that huge school on her own while a gang of girls were picking on her. It made her want to scoop Poppy up and tell her that she never had to go back there, though such a thing wasn't possible. Had one of those girls smashed Poppy's phone?

"Okay, thanks for telling me. And thanks for taking care of her as well. You know I appreciate it."

"Of course." Tasha gave her a sympathetic smile. "And while I don't want to tell you how to parent Poppy, just try not to be too hard on her about the smashed phone, okay? She was pretty upset about it earlier. She's been having a rough time with all the changes going on in her life."

"No, I know. I won't."

She leaned in and gave her sister a quick hug and then shouted up the stairs for Poppy to come down.

Poppy appeared, dragging her school bag down the stairs behind her.

"Hey, kiddo," Erica said, trying to keep her tone bright. "Aunty Tasha says your phone got smashed."

"Yeah, don't be mad. It wasn't my fault."

Erica put her arm around Poppy's skinny shoulders. "I'm not mad. Accidents happen."

She gave Natasha another grateful smile, bundled Poppy into her coat, and then guided her out of the door.

They drove home in near silence. Erica did her best to ask Poppy about her day but only received one-word responses.

When they got back into the house, Erica said, "There's a place next to the Tube station that replaces phone screens. How about we go before school tomorrow morning?"

Poppy stood still. "But it's going to cost you lots of money."

"It doesn't matter. It's only money. And it's the first time you've done something like this. Just make sure you're more careful in the future."

"I was careful!" she protested.

"Well, if the screen got broken, you weren't that careful."

"It was an accident! Don't you ever have accidents? The whole point of an accident is that it's something you can't help. No one does it on purpose."

"Okay, okay. I was just saying."

Poppy folded her arms. "Fine. Whatever."

She remembered what Tasha had said about feeling like something was off.

"Poppy, if something happened that upset you, you'd talk to me, right?"

"There's nothing to talk about."

"Did someone else break your phone? You know it's part of my job to be able to know when someone is lying to me."

Poppy rolled her eyes. "Yeah, just what I need. You playing detective on me. Why don't you just put me in handcuffs and lock me in a cell and be done with it."

"Don't be so silly—"

"I am not being silly! You've got no idea what it's like being me." She was boiling with her fury, her face bright red. "All my life I've had other kids making comments because my mum is a detective. They say stupid stuff like 'ooh, are you going to get your mum to arrest me?' And the teachers all act like I should be something special just because of your job. Like maybe I'm not as smart as you, or as pretty as you!"

Erica's jaw dropped. She had no idea where all this was coming from. "Poppy, sweetheart, you are way smarter and prettier than I have ever been."

Poppy's eyes shone with tears. "No, I'm not. I'm nothing to nobody."

"How can you say that? You're my entire world."

"Don't lie, Mum. We both know that's not true."

"You want me to quit my job? Then fine, I'll do it. Because you know what, Poppy, I can live without my job, but I could never live without you. You are the most important thing in my life. Nothing else comes close."

Poppy lowered her head. "I don't want you to quit your job."

"Do you want me to speak to the school?"

Her head shot back up, her eyes round with alarm. "No! Don't do that! You'll only make things worse."

"What am I making worse, Pops? Are you having trouble with some girls at school? Are they who broke your phone?"

She wouldn't meet Erica's eye. "No, I told you already. I don't know how it got broken. It just did, okay?"

Erica struggled with what was the right thing to do. She didn't want to go behind Poppy's back, but she also wanted to do something. She also needed Poppy to know that this wasn't her fight to handle and that she could rely on Erica to deal with things.

The problem was that Poppy didn't feel that she could rely on her mother at all.

TWENTY-SEVEN

Neve went home and searched up the name of the young woman, Lindsey, together with the word 'suicide' and the approximate date the woman in the café had told her that this other woman had taken her own life.

It took a little bit of digging, but eventually, she found the woman's profile. She didn't have a surname attached to it, but instead had used her first name twice.

Neve's heart stuttered, and for a second, she found she couldn't breathe. She could have been staring at a younger version of herself. The photograph that she'd been shown in the café hadn't caught it in the way this picture did. The young woman seemed happy, staring directly into the camera, her wide smile revealing straight white teeth. There must have been a breeze when the photograph was being taken as her brown curls whipped around her face, and she had one hand lifted to hook one away from her cheek.

Stupidly, Neve's first thought was that this woman was too young for Guy. But then maybe Guy had lied about his age? Had he lied to her, or had he lied to this girl? Or perhaps it was Neve who was too old for Guy?

She shook the thought from her head. None of that mattered. What mattered was that a young woman was dead and apparently Guy was to blame.

She kept scrolling, reading all the comments that had been posted on her wall from well-meaning friends and associates. So many saying 'I'll miss you' and 'so tragic' and 'too young' and 'hope she's at peace now'.

Neve found her eyes welling with tears.

This poor woman. She couldn't imagine ever being so desperate that she would choose to take her own life, no matter how bad things got. She remembered after her husband had thrown at her that he didn't love her anymore, how it had come completely out of the blue and blindsided her, that she'd been in a very dark place. The future she'd taken for granted had been ripped out from under her. But she'd never once considered doing something as final as taking her own life.

She couldn't have done something like that to her friends and family either.

But then she guessed that meant she'd never been in such a dark hole as this other woman had been. A dark hole that Guy had apparently put her in.

She imagined how heartbroken her daughter would be. No wonder the woman was hellbent on protecting others from Guy.

Neve continued to scroll, trying to learn everything she could about Lindsey. She searched all of her photographs, a part of her hoping to find one of her and Guy together, while also praying she wouldn't find one. Had all those photographs been deleted? She couldn't imagine her family would have still wanted them up to see whenever they visited her page on the internet, the two of them looking happy after what had happened.

Still, she would have felt better if she'd found a photograph—some kind of evidence, other than her suicide, that they'd been together. It would have made it all more real for her.

Perhaps she was Googling the wrong person? It should be Guy who she was obsessively reading about, not his victim.

Or maybe it should be the woman who'd been stalking her who she should be digging into.

A moment of inspiration hit her. If the woman had been friends with Lindsey's sister, perhaps she'd show up as a mutual friend. If she did, then Neve would at least have a name she could use to delve into her further.

She pulled up all the friends still remaining on the profile and scanned them, first to see if any were obviously the dead woman's sister, and then to see if any were the woman who'd been stalking her. But there were hundreds of different profiles, and it was near impossible to check them all. Plenty didn't even have photographs as their profile pictures and instead used random avatars.

She went back to the woman's wall and tried to see if any of the comments said something like 'I'll miss you forever, sis', but there was nothing written like that. If anything had been left at the time of her death, it had since been deleted.

"Shit," Neve cursed.

She needed to leave to meet Guy shortly. He'd sent her a message saying he missed her and couldn't wait to see her, but she hadn't replied. Something that would have made her giddy only this morning, now filled her with dread.

She had to go through with it. She needed to see him again, and look him in the eye, and try to ascertain for herself if he was the person that woman had made him out to be.

HE WAS ALREADY WAITING for her at the restaurant when she arrived.

A part of her had expected him to be changed somehow. That she'd come face to face with him and see someone different. But he was exactly the same handsome, attentive man, and he seemed so happy to see her.

He stood from the table and kissed her on the mouth.

"You look beautiful this evening," he told her.

She smiled, and, to her relief, it didn't even feel forced. "Thanks. You're not so bad yourself."

While she'd been away from him, she'd allowed the strange woman to grow stronger in her head, but now she was with him, that power faded and she found herself siding with Guy.

Why should she believe some stranger over him?

But only moments later, she found herself flip-flopping again. Was Guy a conman and this was all an act?

The waitress came around to take their order. Neve went for the mushroom risotto and a sparkling water. Guy ordered a pizza and a pint of lager.

To all intents and purposes, they seemed like a normal, happy couple, but she had a buzzing inside her head that she couldn't silence.

How was she supposed to act normally? This whole thing was crazy. She should just confront him and ask him outright?

But what would he say if she did? He wasn't going to admit to anything, was he? He'd just say the woman was lying.

He reached across the table and took her hand. "Is everything okay, Neve? You're unusually quiet."

God, she should have cancelled. She should have said she wasn't feeling well and she needed an early night. He was the type of man to offer to come around and bring her soup or something, though.

Or was he? Was it all just an act?

She couldn't help thinking of the woman's sister, the one who'd killed herself, and a surge of anger rose inside her. Was she really dead because of what this man sitting across the table from her now, holding her hand, had done to her? If she mentioned something, would he just vanish?

"I'm sorry. I've got a headache. I should have cancelled."

"I didn't realise you weren't feeling well. We don't need to have dinner. I can order you a taxi?"

"No, no. I brought my car. I hadn't planned on drinking anyway...because of the headache."

What she really meant was that she hadn't wanted to drink alcohol because she'd wanted to have the car available in case she needed to make a quick escape. Plus, she needed to keep her wits about her. A couple of glasses of wine, and she knew she wouldn't be thinking straight. After what had happened today, she wanted to keep a clear head.

There was still a part of her that questioned what the woman had said, however. She'd checked up on him online as soon as she'd got the request for a date, and nothing unusual or suspicious had come up. There had been a couple of profiles on social media platforms that weren't used regularly, and a local newspaper article about people in business, but there hadn't been anything alarming.

Hadn't that been what the woman had said, though—that they deliberately sprinkled bits about themselves over the internet to make it seem more convincing? Was that what Guy had done? Were none of the profiles or articles real?

"Do you want to call it a night then?" he asked.

She remembered the risotto. She hadn't eaten her lunch either today, so she was actually starving.

"No, we've ordered now. I might as well eat. Then I'll call it an early night."

"Of course, whatever you want."

She sat anxiously chewing on a nail, waiting for her food to arrive. She hoped he'd take the excuse of a headache as an explanation for her quietness. He chattered on, filling in all the silent spaces, allowing her to just give a murmur of understanding or the occasional nod and smile as a response.

The food arrived, and Neve ate quickly. She had been famished, and the risotto was cooked to perfection. That this would have been a perfect date night if she'd never met the woman in the café made her want to cry.

Guy paid the bill and then walked her to her car.

He leaned in to kiss her cheek, and she stiffened.

He drew back and eyed her, concerned. "Are you sure everything is okay?"

Well, no, Guy. I was told today that you're a con artist and you're responsible for a woman killing herself, so actually, everything isn't okay.

She kept the words clamped between her lips. If she told him, he'd be gone, and then some other poor woman would fall victim to his charms. Because he was charming, wasn't he? He was funny, and thoughtful, and generous. He was everything she'd hoped to find in a man, and, instead of being happy, she was questioning it all. She wished she'd never met the other woman, that she could have lived in ignorant bliss. But then she didn't really want that, did she? She didn't want to get however many months down the line, and turn around, and realise she'd given him all her money and that he wasn't who he'd said he was.

"Yes, like I said—just a headache. I'm sorry for not being better company."

"That's okay. I hope you feel better tomorrow."

"Me, too."

Neve climbed into her car and drove home. There was nowhere to park outside her house, so she had to find an empty space down the road.

She was just about to walk towards her house when she remembered that they'd used the last of the milk in the tea this morning. Damn.

The cupboards were bare, and she didn't even have anything in for breakfast either. She no longer bothered with doing big shops, and she often only had the basics in. That was another part of living alone that she'd thought she'd appreciate, but actually she'd missed. She'd thought she'd hated all those years of cooking for a family, of trying to manage everyone's likes and dislikes, while rarely considering her own. At the time, she'd thought it was going to be the world's greatest luxury to eat whatever she wanted, when she'd wanted. But the reality had been very different. Instead, she'd found she could never be bothered to make an effort. She still liked making a roast when her daughter came around for dinner, but when it was just her, she survived on toast and omelettes and the occasional microwave meal. She didn't even have those things in right now, so if she was going to have a cup of tea in the morning, she was going to need to stop at the local shop.

A weary sigh fell from her lips. She felt heavy from her heartbreak and didn't have the energy to do much of anything at all.

Heartbroken. How could she be such a thing at her age? She was too old for all this crap. Besides, she barely knew the man. He hadn't been in her life for long. There was no way she should have anything that came close to real feelings for him. It had been more the possibility of it all that she'd fallen for. The idea of finally being in a real relationship again.

She didn't even want to confide in her daughter. It wasn't as though anything had really happened, but she was still embarrassed and ashamed.

Was that how the poor woman who'd killed herself had felt? Neve's heart went out to a woman she'd never even met.

She slipped inside the corner shop, run by a Turkish couple. The familiar scent of unusual spices, slightly musty, mixed with baked bread hit her nostrils. They had a deli counter at the back that sold olives and hummus and fresh bread in the mornings. At this time, there were only a few loaves left, wrapped in plastic to be taken up to the till. She grabbed a basket and added one of the loaves so she could make toast in the morning, then went to the small fridge for a pint of milk—she didn't need any more than that, it went off otherwise—and thought *fuck it*, and put in a bottle of white wine as well.

She rounded one of the aisles and stopped short.

"Neve," the man said. "What are you doing here?"

For a split second, she struggled to place him. It was stupid, since they'd worked together for years, but it was seeing him out of the office and no longer in a shirt and tie that had confused her.

"Nigel!" *Nasty Nigel, Naughty Nigel, Nitpicky Nigel...* "I should ask you the same question."

He lifted his blue plastic basket as a way of explanation. "Just popping in to get a couple of things."

She peered into the empty basket. "You've not done very well so far."

He chuckled. "Just getting started. What are you up to?"

"Grabbing some milk." She frowned. "I didn't think you lived around here." She couldn't recall exactly where he lived, but she was sure it was on the other side of the river.

"No, I don't. I was just visiting a friend."

His gaze skimmed away from her, and a thought popped into her head.

He's lying.

Had he followed her? Had he picked up the basket after she had as an excuse as to why he was in here? Was this some weird way of orchestrating a meetup outside of work? He had repeatedly asked her to go on a date, even though he was her boss, and technically she could have reported him to HR.

"If you haven't had dinner yet," he said hesitantly, "there's a great Italian down the road. Their meatballs are incredible."

After the day she'd had, she couldn't help herself. "Did you follow me in here to ask me that, Nigel? You know that could be construed as harassment? Stalking even?"

He blushed right to the roots of his hair, even the tips of his ears turned puce. "What? God, no. Of course not. I-I'd never do that."

"Really? Who is your friend then? Where do they live?"

"A couple of streets from here. We went to school together." He took his phone out of his pocket. "You can call him, if you want. Ask for his address. He'll confirm that what I'm telling you is the truth."

Doubt slid through her, knotting her stomach. Fuck, was he telling the truth? Oh my God, had she just accused her boss of stalking her?

Now it was her turn to go red. "No, no, it's fine. Shit, I'm sorry. I've just had a really bad day. Please, can we forget the last five minutes ever happened?" Her cheeks burned, and she couldn't meet his eye. How the hell was she going to be able to face him at work?

He pocketed the phone again. "Yeah, of course. I'm sorry about the misunderstanding."

"No, it's my fault. I'd better get going." She nodded towards the counter.

A part of her was tempted to just dump the basket and make a run for it. She didn't think she'd ever been so mortified in her entire life. But she thought that would make her seem even more unhinged, so she forced herself to walk to the counter and pay for the few items she had in her basket. The entire time the young woman behind the till was ringing them up, Neve was hugely conscious of Nigel's presence in the shop. She prayed he wasn't going to finish his shopping and line up behind her. She hoped he'd want to avoid her right now as much as she wanted to avoid him.

Thankfully, the items were rung up fast and placed into a reusable carrier bag, and then Neve was able to get the hell out of there.

It wasn't until she was at her front door, putting the key in the lock, that she remembered how quickly Nigel had put the phone back into his pocket. He hadn't pressed her to check up on the friend and make sure the story was real. Was that because he'd been betting on her embarrassment and so refusing? Had it been a bluff?

She paused, her stomach churning.

She wanted to cry. What was she supposed to believe? How could she trust anyone now?

TWENTY-EIGHT

Erica left the house early the following morning, promising she'd take Poppy to the place next to the Tube station to fix her phone before she took her to school. It meant she'd be late into the office, but her team could handle her absence for an hour or two.

What she hadn't told Poppy was that she'd also made an appointment to speak to the head of year. She knew her daughter would object, but Erica felt like she didn't have any choice. She couldn't just sit back and let her daughter be bullied—if that's what was even happening.

They reached the small booth that replaced phone screens, as well as sold covers and pop-sockets. Erica left the broken phone with the young man behind the counter and tried not to wince at the seventy quid it would cost her. They had an hour before it would be ready, so they nipped into the coffee shop next door. She treated them both to a coffee—Poppy opting for something that looked more like a desert than a drink—and a couple of pastries for breakfast.

Poppy seemed a little happier that morning, and Erica

took comfort in that. Maybe they were past the worst of things and it would start settling down. All she wanted was for her daughter to be happy, and seeing her so upset all the time, and feeling completely helpless to do anything about it, troubled her.

Just as they finished their breakfast, Erica got a text to say the phone was ready to be collected. They went back to the booth to find the man fixing it had it as good as new and had even put a screen protector on the phone.

"Okay?" Erica handed the phone back over to Poppy. "Happy now?"

Poppy nodded. "Thanks, Mum."

"Make sure you take care of it this time."

"I will."

She drove her into school. Poppy didn't want to be seen with her mother, so Erica didn't walk her in. She just dropped her off and watched her daughter join the stream of identically dressed children and then vanish inside the school gates.

Erica waited for a moment and then found somewhere to park. She didn't want Poppy to see her following her in. As soon as the bell rang, Poppy would be in her tutor class, so she wouldn't see Erica slipping inside the school as well. If she'd still been at primary school, Erica would have worried about one of Poppy's friends spotting her, but since she didn't even know who Poppy's friends were at high school, it wasn't something she worried about. No one here knew who she was.

She climbed out of the car and headed into the building. She stopped at the reception area and gave her name and who she was there to meet. The receptionist told her to take a seat, which she did. While she was waiting, she checked her phone, making sure no one from the office had called her with anything urgent. They hadn't. She didn't know if she should be relieved or disappointed. They could really do with a break in this case.

"Mrs Swift?"

The male voice came from above her, and she glanced up to find a young man in a shirt and grey trousers standing in front of her.

Erica got her feet. "Yes, hi."

"I'm Mr McNally, the head of year seven."

She put out her hand to shake his. "Mr McNally, thank you for seeing me on such short notice. Poppy doesn't know that I'm here, and I'd like to keep it that way."

God, when did teachers start looking so young? He was the head of year, but she wouldn't have been surprised if he hadn't left school himself not long ago.

"Do you want to come through?"

She followed him down the corridors and into an office. She had no idea if it was his office, or just a private place where he'd decided they could talk.

She pushed a stray strand of hair out of her eyes. "Thank you for seeing me so quickly."

"Of course. We take accusations of bullying extremely seriously."

"It's not an accusation, exactly," she said. "I mean, Poppy hasn't said as much to me directly. It's more of a gut instinct. She hasn't been herself since starting here."

He cleared his throat. "I have actually spoken to Poppy—not today, obviously, as there hasn't been time— but over the last couple of weeks when other teachers mentioned to me that she seemed unhappy."

"Yes, and that does seem to have coincided with her starting a new school."

He drew a breath and then released it again. "The thing is, Mrs Swift, when I've spoken to Poppy, it's not just about the school. It's normal for kids to struggle between the transition of going from a primary school to a secondary school, but often the way they deal with it is by having a solid base at home. But Poppy tells me there's been a lot of change there, too. There's been a breakup, I understand, and the loss of a pregnancy."

Erica winced. "I didn't realise she'd talked about that."

His cheeks stained with colour. "I'm sorry, I didn't mean to bring up something painful."

"No, you're right. Those have been things Poppy has been needing to deal with as well, but I don't think that's the only thing that's wrong."

"But it could certainly be having an impact on her mental health," he insisted.

Erica ground her teeth. "Are you saying that the school is taking no responsibility for how Poppy is feeling?"

"I'm saying that we'll keep an eye on Poppy, and those around her, but that you can't just put all the blame onto the school."

She found herself getting defensive. "She came home with a smashed phone yesterday but refused to tell us what happened."

He shrugged. "Children break their phones and don't tell their parents about it. I'm afraid there's nothing unusual about that. It is the reason we advise them to leave their phones at home."

She had to stop herself rolling her eyes. "It's not that easy, in this day and age."

"Tell me about it. I'd prefer to ban them from schools

altogether, but then we have outrage from the parents saying they can't get in touch with their children all day." He let out a sigh. "Look, if Poppy has any further issues, tell her to come and speak to me."

He was trying to dismiss her, but Erica wasn't going to let things drop so easily. "Her cousins say that there are some mean girls who have been teasing Poppy. Do you know anything about that?"

"These first few weeks are all about the kids trying to find their footing. It's like they're creating a pecking order."

"Right, and my daughter is at the bottom of it," she threw back bitterly.

He raised a hand. "That's not what I meant. It's more that we expect this time to have a little turmoil. It's normal. I'm sure Poppy will come out the other end with a new group of friends and a new standing in the world."

They were both being defensive—her of her home life, and him of the school—and stuck in the middle of them was Poppy.

She drew a breath and forced a smile. "Let's hope you're right."

He got to his feet, a clear indication that the conversation was over. "I'm sure Poppy will have an enjoyable and successful time here."

Why did she feel like he said that to all the parents?

SHE GOT BACK into the office and headed straight for the coffee machine.

Shawn caught up with her. "Everything okay?"

Maybe she should confide in him about Poppy having

problems, but she worried it would sound as though she was, in part at least, blaming him. Their relationship always seemed to be walking a precarious line, and she didn't want to do or say anything that might tip it over the edge. Perhaps Poppy would open up to Shawn, however.

Right now, she needed to get her head back into work.

She plucked the cup out of the holder. "Yeah, fine. Have I missed anything important this morning?"

He seemed to accept this. "So, I've just spoken to Jasmin, and she's sent over something she's found on Darren Blanton's phone. He has a secret messaging app on there. It took her a little while to crack it, but she has now."

"Secret messaging? Outside of the dating apps you mean?"

"Yes, it's more like a messaging app, except when you check the phone, it actually looks like it's nothing more nefarious than a calculator app. But when you go into the app and enter a certain code number, it turns into a messaging app."

"Well, shit. I didn't even know that existed."

"Yeah, it's pretty smart. But here's the thing. It's not other women he'd been talking to. It's other men."

She angled her head with interest. "Men? Did he swing that way, too?"

"No, not like that. These messages are more like...like they're colleagues. They're all about women, what to do to get them onside, how to make them trust you, that kind of thing."

She paused. "Like a forum on how to con women?"

"Exactly. It's all been uploaded so you can see for yourself."

"Who are these people? Can we track them down?"

He made a face. "No more than we can track down the women Guy had been talking to online."

She took her coffee over to her desk and settled down to read the messages. There were twelve different profiles who were exchanging information. The more she delved into the conversations, the more depressed she got. It was hard to imagine how women trusted anyone. It was all about manipulation, how they could use words and actions to get the woman to believe them, and then they'd do and say what the man wanted. They had lists of common situations that might trip them up—such as the woman wanting to go to his house instead of always being at hers—and ways these could be combatted. There were other tips and advice: Always dress smart, but never be too formal. Make sure you smell good. Dirty nails are a sign of a man who doesn't take care of himself.

There were even parts that discussed how to touch a woman—to always cup their face before kissing them, looking into their eyes for permission, and then to lace your fingers in their hair—and reading them turned Erica's stomach.

It was a how-to manual for getting a woman to fall for a man, except these men weren't interested in the woman's heart. They were only interested in their bank balances.

Bank accounts were also something that were discussed at great length. Once a person had gained access to their victim's home, hidden cameras could be set above desks to capture login details and security information for bank accounts. But mostly it was discussions about how this was a long game, and how, if they followed all the correct steps, these women would willingly be throwing money at them.

Erica kept reading, despite her distaste, but when the conversation turned away from manipulation and was more to do with the fact one of their members had apparently disappeared, she paused and refocused with fresh eyes.

There was lots of speculation on what had happened to him. Then one person commented that he hoped his missus hadn't stabbed him, that maybe he'd got busted, 'cause he'd been Scottish and there had been a report of a man of a similar age being murdered overnight.

Erica paid attention to this. It had a similar feel to it as what had happened to Darren Blanton. A man being killed overnight in his home. Something about it called to her. She glanced to the date of the messages. They'd been sent three years ago. Jesus Christ. How long had these people been working to con women for?

She leaned out from her desk, rolling back slightly on the wheels of her chair. "Hey, Lewis, can I get you to look into a past case for me? Would have happened in July three years ago, most likely in Scotland. A man, middle-aged, but I'm just guessing at that, was stabbed overnight in his home."

"Any idea what part of Scotland?" the young DC asked.

"No, sorry. I'll let you know if I come across anything else."

"No problem."

Could this be a link? Had it happened before?

Two men in this secret chat could now be dead. Who were the others? Were they potentially other victims, or could they even be suspects?

There was also still the possibility that Darren's death had nothing to do what he was getting up to on the side, but, somehow, the more she dug into this, the more that seemed unlikely. They'd checked out the alibi of Cole Seger, but there were the two other men he'd been with that night who they didn't yet have names or alibis for. Or maybe the person responsible was someone else entirely? The dive team hadn't found a gun yet either. A few more hours and they'd give up.

Could the shooter have kept the weapon with them? What reason would they have for doing that? In Erica's mind, it was like keeping hold of a neon flashing sign that read 'guilty'.

Unless, of course, they'd kept hold of the weapon because they planned to use it again.

TWENTY-NINE

Later that afternoon, Lewis waved a sheaf of papers he'd printed out in her direction.

She tried not to focus in on his bruises. She hadn't pushed him again to investigate the two men who'd attacked him, though she still believed that they should. Not only for Lewis's sake, but for whoever their next victim might be. In her experience, men who liked to beat up people for fun didn't just stop willingly.

"Boss, I think I've found something," he said. "A murder that took place in Glasgow around the date you suggested. The victim's name was Gordon Smiley."

"Interesting name," Erica said.

"Well, Mr Smiley was killed in his home by an intruder. Not a gunshot this time. The killer used a knife, and a big one. He was stabbed in the back, which punctured a lung. He effectively drowned in his own blood."

"Did they catch anyone for it?"

"Nope. Whoever is responsible is still a free man. But here's the thing. Just like in our case, whoever stabbed him just walked right in there in the middle of the night. There was no sign of a break-in or even anything stolen."

"What about family? Was he home alone at the time of the murder?"

"His partner was asleep in bed. She didn't find him until the morning, and, by then, it was too late."

Erica narrowed her eyes. "You mean she didn't hear him being stabbed? Did she hear a struggle, or him calling for help, or anything?"

Lewis checked the notes. "According to her statement, she said she sleeps badly, and she'd taken a sleeping tablet that night. She said she also wears earplugs and a sleep mask because if something wakes her up at night, she can never get back to sleep. Of course, in her statement, she deeply regrets that now."

"Are we able to speak to her, or speak to one of the detectives on the case?"

"She's moved abroad, as far as we can tell. Definitely not in the area anymore, though who could blame her for moving after that? I'll try and get in touch with the SIO on the case and see if there's anything they can help with. Maybe something about our case will ring a bell with them."

Was this person connected to Darren Blanton?

"Maybe we can find a phone number or email for the partner, too. Even if she's abroad, she still might have left a contact for post to be forwarded to her or something. See who she sold the house to as well. They might have forwarding details."

"Will do, boss."

If this wasn't an unrelated incident, what did it mean? That someone was killing men connected to the secret chat group where they were passing on tips about how to scam women? Could it be a rival, or someone else entirely?

THIRTY

Neve had spent most of her morning at work doing her best to avoid Nasty Nigel, while being hugely conscious of the fact he was in the same building as her. Though he'd come up with an explanation about why he'd bumped into her last night, the whole incident had left her uneasy, and that, combined with everything else that was going on, created a perfect storm of anxiety.

She'd barely slept the night before, tossing and turning, and going over everything again and again. When her alarm had eventually gone off, she'd dragged herself out of bed, bleary and overemotional, and feeling as though she'd had no rest at all.

She'd been tempted to call in sick, but she had too much work on. She also didn't want Nigel to think she was calling in sick purely because of him, so she'd forced herself into the office.

Mid-morning, she nipped out of work to drop one of her suits at the dry cleaners. She was standing on the street outside the shop when a female voice spoke from behind her.

"Have you given any thought to what I told you?"

"Jesus Christ." Neve clutched her hand to her chest and spun around to face her. "I'm starting to feel like everyone has turned into a goddamned stalker."

Her eyes narrowed. "What are you talking about?"

Neve shook her head. "Never mind."

"Did you look up my friend's sister, Lindsey? I assumed you'd Google the story I told you."

"I did. She was so young. Only thirty-six. I'm so sorry. It's truly tragic."

A knot formed in Neve's throat at the memory of reading all the comments on the dead woman's social media wall.

"So you know I'm telling you the truth, and the man responsible is walking around, living his life as though nothing has happened." She paused and pressed her lips together. "Did you see him last night?"

"Yes, but I didn't stay long. I made an excuse, and said I had a headache, and left. I couldn't just sit across a table from him, acting like everything was all right, when it clearly wasn't. I'm not that good an actress."

"You need to try," she said. "Just until we can come up with a plan. We need to know where he's going to be and when. It's important."

A couple of words jarred in Neve's head. "Wait a minute. Who is we? And what kind of plan are you talking about?"

"We're the people who are working to take bastards like Guy down. I already told you this, Neve. The police do nothing, so we're left with no choice. Do you know how many women are scammed out of money by men like him every year? More than we'll ever know about because so many of the women are too embarrassed and ashamed to even admit that they've fallen for it. These men reach out to the most susceptible of people and play with their most vulnerable part—their hearts." Her voice rose as she spoke. "It's utterly, utterly cruel, and I'm sick to fucking death of these sons of bitches getting away with it."

The woman drew a breath, and the new silence settled around Neve's ears like snow.

When Neve eventually spoke, she did so in a much quieter voice. "So...what is it you do to stop them?"

"You don't need to worry about that right now. Like I said, just keep Guy close. Let us deal with the rest."

"What if he gets suspicious? Or decides that I'm too much work?"

"He won't."

It occurred to her that if this was all true, then she might not be the only woman who Guy was 'playing' right now. He might have a few on the go. The thought made her heart ache. To think she'd believed they'd had some kind of special connection. Did every woman he got involved with feel the same way? Was that what made him so good at this?

He'd been blessed with twinkling blue eyes and a cheeky smile, and he used it to con naïve women out of their savings.

"But what's your plan?" she pressed. "Are we collecting information on these men to give to the police? How's that going to work? If I know what he is, and what he does, I'm not just going to send him my money. And it's not exactly illegal for him to ask me for any either, is it?"

"That's the problem. These women are being coerced, but if they're not actually stealing the money from them, if the women are sending the money apparently willingly, it's a lot harder to prove."

"You still haven't answered my question."

The woman took hold of the top of Neve's arm and drew her closer, so she could drop her voice to just above a whisper. "All you need to do is make sure Guy is at your place, and that you leave the front door unlocked. If you have any security cameras, turn them off, too, or at least don't charge them or make sure they're facing the wrong way."

Alarm slammed into Neve's chest. "Why? What are you going to do?"

"You don't need to know about that, okay? Just remember what this man has done, and what he's capable of doing if we carry on doing nothing."

Neve's stomach churned. "I'm not sure about this."

The woman lowered her grip and took her hand, squeezing it tight. The grip was verging on painful. "This isn't the time to be wishy-washy about things. Whose side are you on? Because we need to know that, Neve. Not just me, but all the women who are in this. If we can't trust you...well, then we'll have to make some different choices."

"What kind of choices?"

Her voice grew low with menace, and her grip grew even tighter. Neve was sure she'd have bruises there tomorrow.

"Choices you won't like. You have a daughter, don't you, Neve? Pretty girl, only twenty years old?" The woman took out her phone and showed Neve a photograph of Chloe. "You know she has her Snapchat location on all the time. I realise she's an adult, but you really need to talk to her about security. It's not safe for complete strangers to see where she is. Men like Guy might take advantage of that."

Neve's mind was spinning. What was this woman really warning her about? Because up until this point, it had been all about Guy, but now she was feeling as though she was the one who was being threatened—well, her and her daughter.

"There are lots of us, Neve. Lots of women who've been screwed over by men, and now we're helping each other. Supporting each other. Going to the police about this won't do a single thing. You'll never know who it is who rids you of him completely. That part will be a mystery to you, and to most of the rest of us, too. That's what keeps us safe. There's no way the police can ever track down who does the deed eventually. There's just too many of us."

Neve swallowed. "Does the deed? Are you talking about killing him? Murder?"

The crazy thing was that the first thought that jumped into her head was that she didn't want it to happen in her home. She didn't want a man to be murdered under her roof. How could she carry on living there if that happened? She'd never be able to come home again. She'd certainly never be able to sleep there. Every time she closed her eyes, she'd picture his face.

"I never said that."

Neve covered her face with her hands. "I'm not a murderer!"

"I'm not asking you to kill anyone. Just create a situation where someone else can take care of things for you. Then you'll be free, and you'll never have to worry about him hurting anyone else."

Free? Was she even trapped? She barely knew the

man. They'd had a handful of dates, that was all. He'd never asked her for money or said or done anything negatively towards her.

"This is insane. I'm sorry, I can't do this."

She suddenly felt as though she couldn't breathe. A tight band wrapped around her chest, and pinpricks of sweat stood out on her brow. She needed to get away from this woman and the craziness she was talking.

Her dry cleaning forgotten, she rushed off, pushing past people on the street in her haste to get away.

The woman's voice chased her.

"Think about your daughter, Neve. How would you feel if it was her?"

This was madness. Neve debated what to do. Should she go to the police and report this woman? But what could she say? That she'd implied that she'd hurt Guy? Or that someone else would? What would the police say to that? Neve didn't even know the woman's name. Shit, she didn't even know if Guy's name was real.

She could warn Guy. Tell him that she knew what he did, and that other women did, too, and if he didn't stop then something terrible was going to happen to him.

How much attention would he pay to that, though? Would he just laugh it off? Or would he take her seriously? One thing she knew for sure was that if all this was true, he would most likely vanish. He'd leave and possibly change his name. He'd be gone, and so would the woman, and none of this would be her problem anymore. And then the woman would be right, and he'd sink his claws into some other unsuspecting victim. What if it was another woman like the sister, someone who was vulnerable, and they chose the same way out by killing themselves? Would Neve then be responsible for their death?

Would that blood be on her hands for not making a different decision?

She wished she had someone to talk to, but how could she tell anyone? If she did allow the strange woman to go through with her plans, then she'd effectively be an accessory to murder.

Except, the woman had never said anything about murder—it was Neve who'd jumped to that conclusion. Perhaps they'd just give him a fright, or warn him off, or maybe steal his wallet, or something.

But what had she meant when she'd talked about her daughter? Had it been a threat to keep quiet? That something bad would happen to her if she dared tell anyone about this? Neve would do anything to protect her daughter—anything.

Even help arrange a murder?

Her phone buzzed, and she glanced down to see a text from Guy. *<Can't wait to see you later.>*

She felt sick. She just wanted this to be over. One way of making that happen was by doing what the woman wanted.

She pushed the thought away. No, that was unthinkable.

With a shaking hand, she quickly typed out a reply. *<I'm sorry, but this isn't working out.>*

She hesitated, wondering if she should add something else. Something that said, 'I know what you are', or even 'watch your back'. But she didn't, and instead hit send. She exhaled a shaky breath. That was the end of it now, wasn't it? She didn't need to worry about the woman going after her daughter, did she?

Could she warn Chloe? How could she without Chloe asking a whole heap of questions that Neve couldn't answer? The woman was just bluffing. She was supposed to be on the side of women, so she wouldn't hurt one of them, would she?

Even so, Neve had thought that sending the text would make her feel better, but it hadn't. If anything, now she felt even worse. She wanted to see her daughter, make sure she was all right.

How would the woman even know that Neve had sent the message to Guy? She couldn't know that. Neve would just tell her that Guy had lost interest in her, that they'd been supposed to have a date, but he hadn't shown. How would she know any differently?

She rang Chloe as she walked back to the office, but it went through to answerphone. She left an awkward message.

"Hi, it's me. Can you call me when you get this? Nothing to worry about!" she added, trying to sound bright, but it came out strained and forced.

Chloe would know right away that something was wrong. She was probably in a lecture and so had her phone switched off. She'd be surrounded by people and would be completely safe.

Was her daughter really in danger from this woman, or even women? How many of them were there? Even if the police were able to find her, they'd have no clue about who anyone else was.

Neve felt as though she'd been backed into a corner. Did she have any choice other than do what had been asked of her?

She covered her face with her hands. No, she wasn't actually considering it, was she?

She must have lost her goddamned mind.

THIRTY-ONE

Erica needed some fresh air—or at least as fresh as it ever got in London.

She stepped outside, lifting her face to the bright autumnal sky and wrapping her arms around herself to keep warm. Her breath froze in tiny clouds in front of her. The streets were busy with traffic. The constant hum that was the background sound of the city.

A too-thin woman with bleached-blonde hair stood on the other side of the road with her back to Erica.

For a split second, the crazy idea that she was looking at a ghost jumped into her head. Maybe it was because the woman was dressed predominantly in white, all except for the brown boots that she'd paired with skin-tight white jeans.

Then, as though she'd sensed Erica standing there, watching her, she slowly turned around.

With a jolt, Erica realised she knew her.

"Victoria," Erica said, drawing to a halt. Instinctively, she hooked her fingers around the strap of her handbag, creating a barrier of her forearm between them. She wasn't sure what it was that made her uncertain of the other woman. "It's freezing out here. Is everything okay?"

The woman's nose and the tips of her ears were bright red from the cold. Erica wanted to wrap her in a scarf and pull a woollen hat over her head. She must be freezing.

"I just wondered if you had an update? I've been so worried..." She wound her hands together in front of her body and chewed anxiously at her lower lip.

"You could have just called."

"It's okay. I needed to get out of the house. It's just all too much."

Erica assumed she meant being at the house when her partner had been murdered there. She could understand that. She remembered after her husband had been murdered, how she'd felt haunted by both him and his killer. Maybe some people would have taken comfort in sensing their dead husband's presence around, but Erica had felt like it had been her fault, and so he'd have blamed her for it. She'd been frightened that he'd want to punish her, which was crazy, because he'd never been that kind of person when he'd been alive—plus, she wasn't someone who believed in ghosts—but that hadn't changed how she'd felt.

Erica frowned. "If it's too much, could you not stay with your son?"

"Yes, I guess so—" Victoria closed her eyes briefly. "I was just hoping for an update, that's all. If you're any closer to finding who's responsible."

"You could have contacted your family liaison officer? You didn't need to come all the way over here when it's so cold."

Victoria gave her head a slight shake. "Yes, you're right. I-I'm not thinking straight."

She had seemed like a nervous, anxious person when Erica had interviewed her, but that was hardly surprising, considering she'd just had her partner die in her arms. How many people *wouldn't* have been like that? But now they were almost a week on from the crime, and, if anything, Victoria seemed worse than ever? Erica was sure the already too-thin woman had lost more weight. If she lost anymore, she'd vanish right before her eyes.

"Let's go inside," Erica said, ushering her back towards the building. "We can talk better in the warmth."

Victoria nodded and allowed Erica to guide her inside. When she was back in the office, she caught Lewis's eye and tried not to flinch at the bruise that was still darkening around it.

"DC Crowe, could you get Ms Nestell a warm drink?"

"Yes, of course."

Erica led her over to her desk and sat her down.

"Are you okay, Victoria? Do you need someone to talk to?"

Grief did strange things to people. Some found it was like having early onset Alzheimer's. They found themselves in places with no recollection of getting there, or walked into a shop and completely forgot what they needed. She'd have expected this more of a couple who'd been married for thirty years, however, or a parent who'd lost a child. Victoria at least now had some kind of idea about what kind of man Darren had been, and they hadn't been together for very long. Perhaps the shock of learning the truth about the man she'd believed she'd loved was part of her grief.

Victoria seemed to almost be sleepwalking. She hadn't met Erica's eye once, and her hands were shaking.

Had she been taking something? Maybe overdone the prescription medication? It wouldn't surprise Erica if Victoria's doctor had prescribed diazepam or something similar, after what had happened.

"Please," Victoria begged her. "Just tell me if you know yet."

"Know who killed Darren?" she checked.

Victoria sniffed and nodded.

She wished she had better news for her. "Not yet, I'm sorry."

Victoria burst into tears. "I just thought you'd have found out by now. Every day that goes by, it gets worse and worse. How am I supposed to go on like this?"

Lewis returned with the tea. He paused next to the sobbing woman, exchanged a glance with Erica, and then set the cup down.

"We really are doing everything we can, Ms Nestell," he said. "We've been working on this case constantly since it happened."

Victoria lifted her watery gaze to his. "Then you think it'll be over soon?"

"We certainly hope so, yes."

It was a promise they were unable to give fully. While they might be making headway, there was always a chance that all of their investigations would lead to a dead end.

THIRTY-TWO

It had felt like the longest day of Neve's life.

Her daughter called her back, reassuring her she was fine. Chloe was more worried about her mother than anything, and Neve had ended up being the one doing the reassuring. Chloe had also been perplexed at her mother's insistence that she turn off her location in her phone.

"What if I lose it and need to find it again?" Chloe had said.

"Please, just humour me. I-I saw a reel about how men are using it to stalk women, and it's got me worried. I'd rather buy you a new phone than worry about some madman tracking you down and throwing you in the back of a van."

She'd practically been able to hear Chloe's eyeroll down the line.

"That's not going to happen, Mum."

"Well, it definitely won't if you turn off your location. Please, Chloe. I know you're an adult now, but that doesn't stop me worrying about you. You're still my little girl."

"Okay, okay. I'm doing it now."

She felt horrible not telling Chloe the full truth of it—that she was concerned it was a woman who'd track Chloe down, instead of a man—but at least she didn't need to worry so much about her daughter now.

Maybe she hadn't needed to worry at all, and she'd misinterpreted what the woman had said as being a threat. After all, she was supposed to be on the side of other women, wasn't she? Even so, her words weighed heavily on Neve's mind.

She dragged herself through the rest of work, her head a constant jumble of warring thoughts, and she hadn't been able to focus on anything she was doing. She'd made mistakes all day and had been distracted by her phone, checking for messages from Chloe, and Guy, and even from the strange woman who's name she didn't even know.

A part of her desperately wanted to hear from him, while the other part of her prayed he'd forget she even existed.

She wished she'd never gone out on that damned date. If only she hadn't responded to his message, none of this would be happening now. She could have been going merrily on her way in her monotonous, if some-what lonely, little life, without the thoughts of suicidal women and stalkers and conmen crowding out her thoughts.

Finally, she made it to the end of her workday.

All she wanted was to go home, shut the door, close all the curtains, and crawl back into bed again.

But as she walked back from the Tube station,

approaching her house, she spotted a figure standing at her front door.

Her heart sank.

Shit. It was Guy.

She drew to an abrupt halt, still standing in the middle of the pavement, several yards from her house. She had the crazy urge to dive between the parked cars and hide there until he eventually gave up and left. But it was literally freezing out, and she couldn't do that without most likely dying of hypothermia.

He must have spotted her as he raised a hand in a wave.

Fuck.

She had no choice but to wave back and then force her feet to move. Dear God, he was standing there clutching a bunch of flowers, a hopeful smile on his handsome face. A couple of white carrier bags hung from each arm, and he raised them as she approached.

"I have flowers, and soup with dumplings, a bottle of wine, and chocolates. I figured that would be covering all bases."

"All bases for what?" she asked.

"Fixing whatever it is I've done wrong." His features tightened with clear confusion. "I thought we had something good, and that you felt the same way. But then almost overnight, it all changed. I can only assume I did or said something that upset you, and whatever it is, I'm sorry. I want to make things right."

He seemed so sincere. It was almost impossible for her to align everything she'd been told with the man standing in front of her. But that was how he worked, she reminded herself. It was because he was such a good actor that what he did got him what he wanted. He fooled the women he was with into believing they were in a real relationship, and then some crisis would come along, and of course they would want to help. They'd want to fix things, to make things better, and they'd tell themselves that money wasn't important. It would probably never even cross their minds that they were being scammed.

She couldn't meet his eye. "I'm sorry, Guy. I just don't see a future for us."

"But why? Was I imagining the chemistry we had? Was it all in my head?"

She was so close to blurting it all out. *Because I know what you are! Because I know you only see pound signs when you look at me. Because you're responsible for another woman taking her own life.*

How would he react if she said all that? Would he deny it? Get angry? Or would he just run?

It was the running part that concerned her the most. If he left and the other woman lost his trail again, she might never find him. Then he'd be free to hurt whoever he wanted for his own gain.

It was so heartless. So cruel. Did he really deserve to have another chance to do this to someone else?

He put down one of the bags and reached out and caught her hand in his. She was so stunned, she didn't even pull away. He stared into her eyes, and for a moment she was lost in their azure depths, as though he was hypnotising her.

"Neve, I never thought I would say this to another person, especially not when we've only known each other such a short time, but I truly believe that I'm falling in love with you."

Her jaw dropped, and she blinked at him. Emotions warred inside her. To think that, if she hadn't been told who he really was, she might be believing him right now. A part of her wanted to. She'd wanted this for so long, had been lonely for so many years, but then that's what he'd seen in her, wasn't it. That's the reason he'd focused on her—well, that and her owning her own home, and working a decent job with a good London salary, and having money in the bank. If she'd been someone in a less stable financial situation, he wouldn't have looked at her twice.

You bastard, she thought. *You utter, utter fucking bastard.*

So instead of telling him exactly what she thought of him, and sending him away to work his magic on someone else, she blinked back tears—that were of anger and frustration rather than the overwhelm of emotion that he most likely took them for—and stepped back.

"In which case, I guess you'd better come in."

THIRTY-THREE

Erica woke to the ringing of her phone.

Instantly, she was alert and reaching for the handset. Shawn's name showed up onscreen, and she swiped to answer.

"There's been another one," he said, without even saying hello. "Man shot in his partner's home just past two a.m. this morning."

She glanced at the red LED lights of her clock. It wasn't even two-thirty yet. She refocused on her phone to see there was a missed call which she must have slept through.

"What's the location?" she asked.

"I'll message it to you. Meet you there."

Fuck. Had a part of her been expecting this after finding out about the Glasgow case? Darren Blanton's murder hadn't just been a one-off.

She got on the phone to her sister to warn her that she was going to drop Poppy off on the way. Natasha would take Poppy to school, so Erica quickly gathered up everything Poppy would need for the morning as well, and then went to wake her daughter. Poppy wouldn't be happy about being made to move beds and houses in the middle of the night, but she was used to it.

Erica arrived on scene thirty minutes later. It was another residential road, much like Victoria Nestell's, and now it was lit up by the flashing blue lights of the emergency services. Though it was still the middle of the night, residents gathered in their doorways or peered out of windows, trying to get an idea about what was going on. Some were even holding up their phones, no doubt recording the scene so they could post about it online.

Shawn was already there, waiting for her. "Morning, boss," he said with a hint of irony. They were nowhere near morning time.

"Do we know who the victim is?" she asked.

"Yes, he's called Guy Thurgood. Fifty-one years old."

"Is this his home address?"

"No. It's the address of his girlfriend, Neve Carter. She was here during the time of the shooting."

Erica looked up at the house. It was a modest semi-detached property. Nothing to indicate why it would have been targeted above any of the other homes. Did it have any security cameras? None were obvious. She checked the neighbour's homes, but again, there was nothing standing out. Still, they might get lucky.

"How did the suspect gain entry?" she asked.

"Exactly the same as with Darren Blanton. They just walked through the door."

Erica paused at this. "They just walked in? Don't most people lock their homes at night?"

"In the city? Yeah, I would have thought so, but

people do get distracted and forget. If the murderer is just trying doors until they find one that's unlocked, it would explain why they haven't needed to break in yet."

"But that it also happens to be the home of a middle-aged couple? And that the man comes downstairs only to be shot while his partner hides away upstairs? Isn't that more than a coincidence?"

Everything about this scene screamed that something was off.

"Are ballistics going to show that the bullet used was the same one as from the Darren Blanton murder?" Erica speculated.

"If it does, it'll explain why the search never showed up a weapon."

"They'd kept the gun because they planned to use it again." Erica blew out a breath. "Where is the partner now?"

"Sitting in the back of one of the response vehicles. She hasn't said a word since the officers were called. I think she's in shock."

Erica glanced over to where two police cars were parked on the road. It was dark so it wasn't easy to see inside, but she could just make out a shadowy figure in one of the rear seats.

"Who made the nine-nine-nine call?"

"She did," Shawn said. "But from the few reports we've managed to get from neighbours, it wasn't made until several minutes after the gunshot was heard."

That could be innocent. Perhaps the woman had frozen, or couldn't find her phone, or, like with Victoria Nestell, she'd been afraid that the shooter had still been around and that she'd become their next victim.

"Any background on her?"

"Nothing in her history. She's a regular, law-abiding citizen, as far as we can tell."

"And what about the victim?"

Shawn shook his head. "Nothing coming up, but it's early days yet. We'll need to do some more digging."

She caught Shawn's eye. "I wonder if there's any chance they met on a dating app?"

"Isn't that how everyone meets these days?" he said. "But yeah, I see where you're heading with this."

Erica wasn't sure if she wanted to take a look at the crime scene first or speak to Neve Carter. She decided to see how much more of the incident reminded her of the Darren Blanton crime scene before she spoke to Ms Carter.

Questions buzzed like angry flies around the inside of Erica's head as she pulled on the protective outerwear, signed in, and ducked beneath the cordon.

Before she entered the property, she glanced over her shoulder at Shawn. "Will you make sure Neve Carter doesn't go anywhere. I'm definitely going to need to speak to her."

"Absolutely."

SOCO were already hard at work inside the house, setting down markers and taking photographs of the scene. She nodded her hellos to the other officers she passed.

The layout of this house was different, so the victim wasn't right at the bottom of the stairs, but instead was lying in the hallway that led to the kitchen at the back of the property. Just like with Darren, he'd been shot in the back. He wore a pair of boxer shorts and a grey t-shirt, which was now stained dark with blood. At an initial glance, there didn't appear to be any defensive wounds on the body.

There was little doubt in Erica's mind that the cases were connected.

She studied the dead man's face. His blue eyes were open and unseeing, but it was still clear that he'd been an attractive man for his age. She didn't want to make assumptions, but it wasn't easy to stop herself.

How similar was this scene to the one in Scotland? Yes, that man, Gordon Smiley, had been stabbed, but otherwise the setup had been the same. Her thoughts went to the woman who'd been at home with him. There must have been a reason the police investigating the case hadn't thought to dig any more deeply into her. With a stabbing, there would have been blood on her body, hair, and clothes. Unless she'd washed and disposed of the clothing before calling the police. Who had made that nine-nine-nine call? Had the murder weapon ever been recovered? She had to assume that the detectives on the case had investigated the partner. They wouldn't have done their job properly otherwise.

Leaving the body, she continued through the house, her keen eye taking in every detail and storing it in the back of her mind.

Flowers had been placed in a vase and positioned on the hall console. Had the victim bought them for Ms Carter? Erica went into the kitchen and checked the bin and the fridge. She found empty takeaway containers in the bin and a finished bottle of wine beside it. Two wine glasses rinsed, most likely the night before, and placed upside down on the draining board.

To any outside observer, the couple had spent a cosy

evening in together, yet in Erica's eyes, everything felt wrong.

Was there anything to indicate which door the trespasser had used? The back door opened onto a garden, which was fenced, with a gate to one side. It would have been a better option as far as not being seen by any of the neighbours.

It had been cold but dry, so the chances of finding footprints in any mud would be slim. What about the frost, though? Frozen blades of grass crushed easily and would leave a trail.

She found a light switch that illuminated the back garden. It was small but tidy, with a paved patio that led directly off the back door. The hulking shape of some garden furniture, covered up for winter, sat to the right, while a pathway made up of stepping stones led to the back gate.

Flicking on the torch app on her phone, she trailed the beam on the ground. If the shooter had been careful, they'd have stuck to the path, but Erica's light picked out a couple of prints in the grass where a foot had missed the stone.

"Can we get some markers out here," she called to the Scenes of Crime officers.

She kept going, reaching the gate and using a gloved hand to open it. It opened onto a narrow alleyway. Was this how the shooter had left the property as well? The fencing was tall enough that it would have shielded them from anyone who might have looked out of a window of any of the adjacent houses, plus it had been dark. Again, she checked for security cameras in the hope the area might be covered. There were none.

The alleyway opened out onto an adjacent road.

Could the intruder have parked a vehicle here and used it to get away? She made a note to get the officers to go door-to-door here as well.

Erica turned to go back to the house.

There was someone she needed to talk to.

THIRTY-FOUR

Neve couldn't stop shaking.

She was sitting in the back of a police car, and the authorities were swarming the street, and her house, like ants.

What the fuck had happened?

This couldn't be real. It couldn't be. She'd gone to sleep and woken up in the middle of a nightmare. No, not a nightmare. A real-life horror story.

Guy was dead. Dead. He'd been bleeding all over her hallway. So much blood. How was it even possible for someone to bleed that much?

He'd been tucked up in bed with her not long ago, their bodies warm and comfortable, and now he was dead.

Maybe she shouldn't have slept with him, but somehow, it hadn't felt wrong. After she'd invited him inside, and they'd opened the wine, and shared the soup, the power that the woman had held over her dissipated once again.

She'd convinced herself that she was just spending

the night with a man she had a connection with. She told herself there was nothing in the way she'd 'forgotten' to lock the front and back door before they'd gone to bed, and, of course, Guy—if that was even his real name— hadn't mentioned it. He didn't live with her, so it wouldn't have so much as crossed his mind to think about something like locking the doors.

He must have heard something during the night and got up to investigate. However, she hadn't heard him get out of bed. The next thing she'd been aware of was waking to the crack of a gunshot. She didn't think she'd ever heard a real gunshot before. It could easily have been a firework going off.

Except she'd known that it hadn't been. Deep down, she'd known.

It hadn't been a surprise when she'd realised Guy was no longer in bed, and she'd crept down the stairs with her heart in her throat, and so much adrenaline coursing through her system that she'd thought she'd pass out from it. She'd known what she was going to find, even though she'd prayed she wouldn't. She wanted to believe that Guy had just snuck out on her.

But then she'd found him lying facedown on the floor, his t-shirt dark with blood.

"Ms Carter?"

She became aware of someone saying her name and blinked up to find a woman staring down at her from the outside of the car. At some point, the door of the police vehicle had been opened, letting the cold night air in, and Neve hadn't even noticed.

The woman was maybe a little younger than her, pretty, with strawberry-blonde hair that had been pulled back into a severe ponytail. Her face was free of makeup and her nose tinged red from the cold.

"Yes?"

The woman produced her ID from somewhere inside her coat. "I'm Detective Swift. I was hoping to have a word with you."

A detective. Fuck. Of course there would be detectives. This would be all over the news now. God, how was she going to explain this to Chloe?

At the thought of her daughter, she burst into tears. Everything was ruined. Her whole life, and probably Chloe's now, too. Everyone would find out about what she'd done. She'd lose her job, her house...she'd end up in prison.

At that, her crying only got stronger.

What a terrible person she was. She wasn't crying in grief over the man she'd helped to kill. No, she was crying over herself and her own stupid little life. She was angry as well, angry that Guy had come into her life, and that he'd brought that woman, albeit inadvertently, with him.

She remembered him telling her that he loved her the previous evening. What a stupid fucking thing to say. They'd barely known each other a week. How was it even possible to know you loved someone after such a short space of time? If he'd only just kept his mouth shut, she wouldn't have taken the drastic step of letting him inside. She'd have just sent him home, as she'd planned.

But it had been that knowledge that he was fucking with her that had been the last straw. He'd believed she'd been stupid and naïve and *lonely* enough to fall for it. How cruel to play with someone's heart in such a way.

The detective was speaking to her, but she had no

idea what was being said, nor did she have it in her to reply.

Neve cried until her pain blocked out the rest of the world.

THIRTY-FIVE

It was clear they weren't going to get anywhere with Neve Carter while she was like this. They were going to need to take her to the station and see if they could calm her down before they could get any information from her.

Her hands had been swabbed at the scene, and they'd taken her clothing as evidence at the station. The house would be searched for the gun, though Erica had a strong feeling they wouldn't find it there.

Erica did her best to rein in her frustration. She was sure the woman knew more than they'd been able to get out of her, which was basically nothing. The suspicious part of her wondered if the hysterical thing was all an act to get out of answering questions, but Neve did seem genuinely distraught.

Closing the car door gently on her again, Erica gave instructions to the uniformed officer to drive Ms Carter to the station.

Hopefully, by the time Erica had finished on the scene, the woman would be in a better state to answer some questions.

In the meantime, she had some other people she could question.

Erica approached one of the neighbours who had been anxiously hanging around at their front door. She was an older woman, who had a dressing gown wrapped tightly around her body and clutched it together at the base of her throat to keep out the cold.

"How well do you know Ms Carter?" Erica asked after introducing herself.

She shrugged. "As well as any of us knows our neighbours. I don't know who the man is, though. I've never seen him before."

"He hasn't been at the house before now?"

"Not that I'm aware of. I saw him waited on her doorstep yesterday evening with a bunch of flowers, but he must be new."

"Does she have many suitors?"

The neighbour gave an uncomfortable laugh. "God, no. Not at all. She was married, years ago, but there hasn't really been anyone since then, as far as I know."

"Is there anyone close to her we can call?"

"She has a daughter—an adult daughter. Her name is Chloe, but I'm afraid I don't have any contact details for her."

"Would any of the other neighbours know them?"

The neighbour grimaced. "I honestly don't know. I'm not sure anyone is that close to her."

On the road, the response car started up, the headlights illuminating the street, and then pulled away from the scene, taking Neve Carter with it.

ERICA PEERED into the interview room back at the station.

Neve didn't seem much calmer than she'd been at the crime scene. She was shaking and sat hunched over, her arms wrapped around her knees. She seemed to be staring at a spot on the floor, her eyes unblinking, though there was nothing of interest there.

Erica wasn't one hundred percent sure how to deal with the woman yet—was she a suspect or a witness?

Erica punched the code into the panel to one side of the door, and the lock buzzed her in. She pushed open the door and stepped inside, her gaze fixed on the woman sitting on the other side of the table, but Neve didn't even register her entry.

She decided to take the softer approach. "Neve, my name is Erica. I understand you're very distressed, but I really do need to ask you some questions about what's happened. Do you understand?"

Still, there was no response.

Erica sat opposite and took her mobile phone out of her suit jacket pocket. "Is there anyone I can call for you? I understand you have a daughter. Chloe, is it?"

For the first time, a flicker of recognition crossed the woman's face.

Erica tried again. "If you give me her number, I can call her right now."

Neve sniffed, and her eyes darted towards Erica. But instead of jumping at the chance to speak to her daughter, Neve shook her head.

"No. I don't want her here. I can't let her see me like this."

"I'm sure she'd want to support you."

"No, please. Don't call her."

Erica pressed her lips together and set the phone down. If she didn't believe the woman might be involved in a murder, she'd have almost felt sorry for her. Why didn't she want her daughter here? What was she trying to protect her from?

"Ms Carter, or can I call you Neve?" Neve nodded to indicate she could. "I'm going to read you your rights now, okay? I need you to listen so I can be sure you've understood them. I'm also going to record this interview."

Neve's gaze flicked up to Erica's, and she gave a tiny nod.

Erica read the woman her rights and then asked if she'd like to have a solicitor present, to which Neve shook her head again.

A knock came at the door, and it opened. Shawn slipped inside and took a seat next to Erica. They shared a look that said 'how's it going?' The slightest twitch of her features conveyed that it wasn't really going anywhere yet.

"Did you see the person who shot Guy, Neve?" Erica asked. "Do you know who did this?"

"I-I-I'm sorry," Neve managed through hitching breaths. "I ca—I just—I—"

"Neve, please, you need to take a couple of deep breaths. We don't understand what you're trying to tell us."

"He's dead, he's actually dead." She covered her face with her hands, her fingers knotting in her hair. "Oh God, this wasn't supposed to happen."

"Are you talking about your boyfriend?"

Neve shook her head. "He-he wasn't my boyfriend. I only met him a week ago."

Erica exchanged a glance with Shawn. So, this wasn't a long-term partner like with Victoria Nestell.

She also seemed unusually hysterical over the loss of a man she'd only known a week and who she didn't consider to even be a boyfriend. But then perhaps it was the violence and shock that had left her in such a state.

Or perhaps she knew more about what had happened than she'd so far revealed.

"Do you know if Guy had any next of kin who we need to inform about his death?" Shawn asked.

"Not that I know of, but how much has what he's told me even the truth?" She gave a strange, strangled laugh. "One time, he told me he was an island—you know, how people say no man is an island? Well, he said that he was. His parents had died years ago, he'd been an only child, and he'd never married or had children. Maybe that should have been a red flag? What kind of person has no one else in their life?"

Erica offered her a sympathetic smile. "Can you talk me through what happened tonight? Start earlier in the evening, from when you got home. Did anything usual happen? Guy doesn't live with you, does he?"

Neve sucked in another shuddery breath and hugged her knees tighter. "I told him it wasn't working. I tried to break things off. I thought I was doing the right thing, but he didn't listen. And then he told me he loved me." She broke down in tears again.

Erica narrowed her eyes. He told her he loved her after only a week? And after she'd tried to break up with him?

"Why did you break up with him?" she asked.

"I didn't trust him."

"What made you not trust him?" Erica pressed.

Neve turned her face away. "How can you trust anyone these days?"

Erica tried a different tack. "Do you know Victoria Nestell? What about a man called Darren Blanton?"

Confusion crossed Neve's features. Her eyes were bloodshot and puffy. "No, I—at least I don't think so."

"Darren Blanton was murdered in a very similar situation a week ago."

Neve's eyes widened. "He was?"

"And we believe a third man in Scotland may have also been murdered in a connected crime."

Neve covered her mouth with her hand. "Oh my God."

"I need you to tell me exactly what happened tonight, Neve."

"I woke to the sound of a gunshot, and I came downstairs and found him like that."

"Do you know the person who shot him?"

Tears streamed down her face. "I hadn't actually thought she'd do it."

Erica felt a jolt of adrenaline at the woman's words. "Who is 'she'?"

"I don't know her. I swear I don't."

Erica remained silent, allowing Neve the time and space to fill in more information, which she did.

"There's this woman...or I think there might be more than one of them. Like a group. An organisation. A syndicate. They're trying to stop men like Guy."

"Men like Guy?"

Neve nodded. "He was never with me because he cared about me. He just saw pound signs. He's done it before, probably many times over. The woman who told me...well, her friend's sister killed herself because of what

Guy did to her. Then she saw that Guy had latched himself on to me, and she wanted to warn me."

"Warn you? But Guy is the one who's ended up dead."

"I know. I didn't know that was going to happen. At least, maybe I didn't want to admit it to myself. But I wasn't the one who shot him, I swear. I was asleep in bed, just like I told you."

"How did this person get into your house, Neve?"

She swallowed hard. "I didn't know what they were going to do. I just didn't lock the door. That was all."

"You left the door unlocked so someone could come into your home during the night?"

She squeezed her eyes shut and nodded.

Shawn said, "For the sake of the tape, Neve Carter has nodded."

Erica softened her voice. "What did you think they were going to do?"

"Take care of him. That's all she said. She never said she was going to shoot him."

"Do you know this woman's name?"

"No, she never told me."

"Did you get any names from the conversations you had together?"

Neve nodded. "Lindsey. I can't remember her surname now, but I found her on social media, or at least I assume it's her. She's the woman who killed herself."

"And she has a connection with this woman?"

"The sister of a friend. But that could be anyone. Lindsey had hundreds of contacts on social media, and I scrolled through them, but I couldn't find the woman who'd spoken to me."

"How did she first make contact with you?"

"She was watching me. Watching me with Guy. She phoned me as well, but the number was always an unregistered one."

Erica looked to Shawn. "We need that phone."

They might be able to trace a number or a message.

He nodded. "I believe it's been taken as evidence."

Erica turned her attention back to Neve. "But you spoke to her in person as well?"

"Yes, a couple of times."

"Can you describe her?"

"In her forties, brown hair. I can't remember what colour her eyes were."

"What sort of build?"

Neve's gaze slipped away as she remembered. "Slim, and maybe five-six."

"Did she have an accent?"

"Just local, I think, but I'm not very good with accents."

"This is all very helpful, Neve, thank you. I'm also going to need the times and places where the two of you met."

She pushed a notepad across the table for the other woman to write them down, which she did.

"Thank you. Let's take a break, shall we?"

Erica cleared her throat and got to her feet. She doubted this would be the last time she'd talk to Neve Carter, but they had enough to get on with, for the moment. She wanted to make sure her team were making progress in what had now become a multiple-murder investigation.

THIRTY-SIX

Erica and Shawn stepped out of the interview room.

"Well, this is a new one," Shawn said. "Conspiracy to murder?"

Erica screwed up her nose. "According to Neve, she didn't know Guy was going to be murdered, but she must have known something bad was going to happen to him for her to have deliberately left the door unlocked. She has no priors and is obviously willing to cooperate with the police to find the person, or persons, who are really to blame—the ones who actually pulled the trigger."

"So, does that make her guilty?"

"I guess that will be up to a jury to decide."

There were the other cases to consider as well; Darren Blanton, and the man up in Scotland. Were there more? They hadn't had the time to go back through cases from years ago, from all over the country, but she guessed it was possible. For as long as internet dating had been going on, women had fallen prey to these kinds of scams. Men had fallen for them, too, it was just that they were far less likely to report it happening.

If what Neve was saying was true, and she was told to ensure there was a way to get into the house, and to stay upstairs, then couldn't it also be true in the case of Victoria Nestell? Was that why Victoria had been acting so strangely? It wasn't that she was grieving—though perhaps she was—it was that she knew exactly what had happened to Darren because she'd been a part of orchestrating it.

Erica suddenly found herself looking at her last interaction with Victoria with new eyes. The woman had begged Erica to tell her if she knew who Darren's killer was yet. What was it Victoria had said? *I thought you'd have found out by now. Every day that goes by, it gets worse and worse. How am I supposed to go on like this?*

Was it not that she'd been begging to know if they'd caught someone, but she'd been begging to know if they'd figured out if she was involved?

Desperate to ease the guilt, she'd wanted to be caught.

Except, it wasn't possible for Victoria to have been the person who shot him. If that had been the case, they'd have arrested her a long time ago. But that didn't mean she wasn't guilty.

Erica called her team into the incident room and filled them in on the huge development that had occurred overnight.

"We know there are other women involved, and, by the sound of things, there's one in particular who is the ringleader. I think if we can find her, then we can start to track down everyone else linked to her. Was she the one who actually pulled the trigger in these murders? I'm not sure, but my gut tells me not. I believe she has a way of manipulating other women, of getting them to do what she wants. She might not have physically shot the gun, or held the knife in the Scottish case, but she was still the driving force." She drew a breath. "We have multiple angles we can tackle this from, but right now our number one focus needs to be identifying the woman Neve was talking about in her interview. We have two locations we can scout for CCTV footage, plus we need to get digital forensics onto Neve Carter's phone as a priority, see if we can trace the calls she's been getting. There's also a social media lead, which is going to take some time to go through, but it needs to be done.

"We need to go back through Darren Blanton's financials, keeping an eye out, in particular, for money he's received as transfers. Let's compare them to whatever we can find with Guy's financial records. They could have a connection. We also need to check Guy's phone. Was he using the same apps as Darren? Is that how these women are tracking the men down? Has one of them infiltrated the secret messaging app and is posing as one of the men? Who was the woman involved in the Scotland case? We need to send local police to pick her up and get on the phone to the detectives working that case. Make sure they know exactly what we're dealing with here. Are we looking for the same person who shot the gun each time? From what Neve Carter has told us, there may be multiple different women involved."

She divided up the actions to each of her team members.

"There's one more important thing," she continued. "We need to bring Victoria Nestell in to be questioned on conspiracy to murder. The last time I saw her, I felt like there was something wrong. I think maybe she was trying to tell me something, but I didn't understand."

"How could you have known?" Shawn said from

where he was sitting. "I'll send some uniformed officers to bring her in."

Erica checked the time. It was gone seven a.m. now. "They'll most likely find her at home, if she hasn't left for work already."

"We'll find her," Shawn confirmed.

THIRTY-SEVEN

Uniformed officers had been to arrest Victoria Nestell and brought her in, but Erica had needed to wait for Victoria's solicitor to arrive before she'd been able to speak with her.

Victoria was sitting in the interview room, openly sobbing, while the solicitor tried to counsel her. She seemed to have shrunk over the past week, and there hadn't been much to her to start with. Now, she was almost childlike, sitting on the other side of the table, clutching tissues in one hand.

Erica and Shawn entered the room, and both took seats opposite Victoria and the solicitor. Erica made sure Victoria had been read her rights and that she was aware the interview was being recorded. For the sake of the recording, she announced the time, the date, their location, and who was present in the room.

"Victoria, do you want to tell us the truth about what happened to Darren? There's been a second murder now, another man, and it's given us reason to believe Darren hadn't just been in the wrong place at the wrong time."

Erica couldn't bring herself to say 'another innocent man'. Had either of these men been innocent? They hadn't had time to dig into Guy Thurgood's past yet, but she had the feeling they'd find a pattern similar to that of Darren Blanton's. Several aliases, money in accounts from various women, a stream of broken hearts, and empty bank accounts left behind him.

"It wasn't me," Victoria said. "I didn't shoot him."

"No, but we think there's a good chance you know who did."

She shook her head. "I don't. It could be anyone."

Erica let out a sigh. "We know how this works, Victoria. We know about Darren's background and how you were approached by a woman who wanted revenge for what he did. We know you conspired with her to ensure Darren was where he needed to be to enable this person to shoot him."

"I only left the door unlocked. That was all." Her voice was barely a whisper.

"And you encouraged him to go downstairs when you heard an intruder, aware of exactly who that intruder was and what they had planned?"

She shook her head. "No, I didn't know who they were. Sh-she never tells us that. It could be anyone."

"Are you saying you don't know the identity of the person who pulled the trigger?"

"No, I don't. There are lots of us. Lots of us women who've been humiliated by these men. None of us know who all the others are. It keeps us safe."

Erica caught Shawn's eye. He had two fingers pressed to his lips, his nostrils flared. She could tell by his serious expression that he was also understanding the scale of what they might be dealing with here.

"But you know the identity of the woman who set it all up?"

"I don't, I swear."

"How did you get in touch with her?"

Victoria dabbed at her eyes with her tissue. "I didn't. She was always the one to approach me."

"Can you describe her?"

Victoria shrugged. "Brown hair, mid-forties, white. She always dressed nicely and was well spoken. I don't know what more to tell you."

"Anything, Victoria," Erica encouraged. "Any detail you can think of that might help us."

She hitched a breath. "B-but that means you'll stop her."

Erica placed her forearms on the table between them. "Men are dead. You can't say that you wish it to continue. I've seen what this has done to you."

"You don't understand how ashamed I was when I learned what Darren had done?" Victoria said. "My son had been telling me for months that Darren was no good, and I'd fought in his corner every time. Then one day, this woman approached me and asked if I knew him and how. Of course, I didn't want to believe her at first, but then she showed me proof. Photographs of him with other women—the women he'd ripped off before me—and the bank transfers they'd made to him. I met one of the women, too. She told me all the same lines he'd used on me, he'd also used on her. It broke my heart."

"So you had him killed?"

She shook her head vehemently, her almost white-blonde hair whipping around her face. "No! I didn't have anything to do with that, not really."

"You knew what they were going to do when they told you to make sure the house had been left unlocked."

"She said they would take care of him, that's all. She never said they would shoot him."

"What did you think would happen?" Erica pressed.

"I-I don't know." Victoria covered her face with her hands. "I was just so angry and upset. I wanted to make him pay for how he treated me...how he treated all the women who came before me."

"So, when we told you about his previous alias, you weren't surprised?"

Victoria lowered her hands again. "I was. I didn't know about that. But I wasn't surprised that he'd do something like that." Her lips vanished into a thin line, and she ducked her head. "If you'd told me a month ago that was the kind of person he was, I'd have accused you of lying, but now I know the truth."

"He might have been a terrible person," Erica said, "but he didn't deserve to die. That's not the society we live in. You should have come to us."

Victoria gave a weak laugh. "And you'd have done what, exactly? Nothing. He'd have claimed I gave that money to him willingly—which, at the time, I did. Maybe a good solicitor could have argued for coercive control or financial abuse, but do you really think he'd have done time for either of those things, and that's if he was even convicted? No, he'd have just changed his name, once again, and gone off to find some other poor woman to screw over."

Erica sighed and sat back. While she would never agree with members of the public acting like vigilantes, taking both crime and punishment into their own hands, she did understand how frustrating it was for victims to watch their abusers just walk away. Erica found it frustrating as well, but that didn't mean she believed she could have someone killed just because they'd hurt another person.

"Victoria, I need you to understand how serious this is. Right now, we'll be asking the Crown Prosecution Service to charge you with conspiracy to murder. That carries a full life sentence. Do you understand that?"

Victoria broke down again, sinking to place her forehead on the backs of her hands that were folded on the table. Her thin shoulders shook. "I didn't know what they were going to do. I didn't. I just wanted him out of my life."

That was going to be for a jury to consider.

"If you help us find whoever was responsible, it's possible a judge will view your case more kindly," Erica said. "That's who we need to find. We believe they, or their associates, may also be responsible for the murder of another man in the early hours of this morning. There also may be a good chance they've done this before. You said you were shown bank statements to prove they'd sent Darren money before. Did you see what the name was on those statements?"

"No, I'm sorry. Those details were blanked out."

Erica didn't point out that if the details were blanked out then those accounts could have belonged to anyone. But then, in this day and age, with Photoshop and other online image software, it was easy enough to change a name on a bank statement.

"Do you at least know what bank it was?"

She sniffed and nodded. "Yes, it was one of the high street ones. Lloyds, I think."

"Do you know the dates the transfers were made?"

"Not exactly, but I think they were from about eighteen months ago."

Erica glanced over at Shawn, who nodded to show he understood why she was going in that line of questioning. If they could find the account under Darren's name, then go back to that date, they might be able to find the deposits, which would in turn lead them to whoever made them.

"Let's take a break," Erica said.

Erica and Shawn stepped out of the room.

Erica blew out a breath and scrubbed her hands over her face. "How many people are we looking for here? Two? Three? Twenty? How many people are involved?"

He cocked an eyebrow. "And by people, do you actually mean women?"

"Yes," she sighed. "I guess I do."

THIRTY-EIGHT

Victoria Nestell wouldn't be walking out of here just yet, if at all. While she was helping with their enquiries, Erica didn't get the same kind of remorse that she felt when she'd been speaking to Neve Carter. Deep down, she thought Victoria believed Darren got what he deserved, and she didn't want them finding the person—or people —responsible.

Erica picked up her cup of coffee and took a sip. It had grown cold, but she didn't have the energy to go to the machine and get a refill. She was running on only a couple of hours' sleep, and there was so much to do, her mind was spinning.

Lewis approached her desk, holding a bunch of print-outs. His bruises had started to turn yellow and green now, and Erica hadn't pressed him any further about finding the men responsible. She'd had her hands full with everything else that had been going on.

"Checking Guy's bank accounts," he said, "it seems he has an irregular income that is based mainly on other people sending him money."

"Other women," Erica guessed.

"We're still tracking down the sender accounts, but that would be my guess."

"Do any of them match accounts that were sending money to Darren?"

"Not that we've found, but, to be honest, that kind of makes sense." The young detective constable sucked air in over his teeth. "If you think about it, these men were all about making their victims believe they were in a loving, committed relationship. I imagine the women involved would only ever allow themselves to fall for it the one time. I doubt they'd be sending multiple men money."

"That's a good point," Erica said. "What about the messaging app? Does Guy's name appear on it? Is it on his phone?"

"Yes, it's on his phone, but he uses an alias."

"Any indication that he's changed his name at any stage like Darren did?

"No, but I assume that's because he doesn't have a criminal conviction like Darren. He must have been confident that his previous victims weren't going to post about him online."

"Because they were too ashamed?"

"Yeah, that would be my assumption."

She didn't want to think ill of the dead, but she had to grind her teeth to prevent herself saying 'that bastard.'

"You know," Lewis said thoughtfully, "some people would say it's only money, and that money's not important in the grand scheme of things. To murder people because someone has been scammed out of a few thousand quid seems pretty extreme."

She considered this for a moment. "If this was a regular crime—say where someone's come along and pinched money out of a purse or stolen a phone—then I could agree with you. But that's not what these people do. They offer up so much more than that, making their victim believe that they're in love, that they've finally found someone special. And then, not only do they learn that it was all a lie and that love never even existed, but they lose their life savings at the same time. The cruelty of it is unimaginable. The heartbreak, the shame, the loss of trust. It's no wonder they do something as final as take their own lives...or take someone else's."

SOMETIME AFTER LUNCH, Jon Howard got her attention. She could tell by his expression that he was excited about something.

"We've got CCTV footage from the café on the day that Neve Carter says the woman approached her. The woman obviously thought there was little chance of us tracking her down, as she hasn't made any effort to hide her face."

"Maybe she thought Neve Carter would never tell. From talking to these women, it seems to me that this person manipulated them into getting what she wanted almost as much as the men who were accused of being con artists."

"It does seem that way, doesn't it? Can coercive control be used to describe this situation as much as it would inside of a home?"

"I'm not sure," Erica admitted, "but I guess it might be something a defence attorney could consider."

She didn't want to admit it, but truthfully, she felt sorry for the two women—Victoria and Neve. They were vulnerable women who'd been put into difficult situations at a time when they were struggling. Of course, they should have come straight to the police, but life wasn't always black and white.

He pushed a printout in front of Erica. "This is the woman who met with Neve. The same one who convinced her to leave her doors unlocked."

Erica stared down at the woman's face.

"I know her."

THIRTY-NINE

Erica sat opposite the woman on the other side of the table.

The last time she'd seen her had been in an overly fashionable office.

It was Anna Moots, one of the managers at Flirty After Forty dating app.

Her dark hair was tied back at her nape, her face free of makeup now, but she sat with her spine ramrod straight and her chin lifted. There was none of the remorse or emotion that the other two women had shown.

Erica had already gone through the routine of reading her rights and offering a solicitor. Ms Moots had refused, saying she had nothing to hide. Erica very much doubted that.

Erica had focused on the wrong app. She'd thought it had been the disguised messaging app that might have been infiltrated and so used to track down which men were targeting which women, but it had been the dating app all along.

"Do you know this woman?" Erica asked, pushing a

photograph of Victoria Nestell across the table. "What about this one?" This time she showed her a picture of Neve Carter.

Anna Moots stared down at the images. "Yeah, I know them."

"You're aware that both of their partners were murdered in their homes?"

Anna snorted. "Partners? Is that what you're calling them. They weren't partners. That implies these men played some kind of equal role. No, these men were leaches. They were parasites sucking off the financial and emotional bloodline of innocent women."

"You don't sound as though there's any love lost there," Erica said.

"I've had more than enough experience with men like that."

"You hate them? Enough to have them killed?"

Anna pulled back her shoulders. "I haven't killed anyone."

"You might not have been the one to shoot the gun, but I believe you're the one pulling the strings."

Anna threw up her hands. "And why would I do that? Plenty of women have had to deal with parasitic men. They don't all go around arranging to have them killed."

From her file, Erica removed printouts from a social media page—the same one Neve had been shown. "The woman who killed herself, that was investigated, just as all unnatural deaths are. It means her DNA is on file, and, when we ran your sample, we got a hit. She wasn't the sister of a friend, was she? She's *your* sister, Lindsey Moots."

Anna's lips pinched. "That doesn't prove anything."

"It gives you motive. A strong one, too."

"Still doesn't prove without doubt that I was the one behind him being killed."

"You got your job at Flirty After Forty after her death. Did someone else put you in that role? Someone pre-arrange it for you?"

"No. It's just a coincidence that I got the job at that time."

Erica pursed her lips and shook her head slowly. "I don't believe in coincidences."

"You can believe what you like, but all I've done is warn women what kind of men they've got involved with. Maybe I've broken some privacy laws by reading the messages between the users of Flirty After Forty, but that's all."

They'd seized Anna's laptop and phone, and Erica hoped that would give them plenty of leads when it came to finding out who else the woman had been in touch with. Was there even someone above Anna? Maybe the person who put Anna in her job?

Erica tried again. "We have people who will attest to the fact that you encouraged these women to leave their doors unlocked so people could gain access to the house to murder their partner."

"I might have said to leave their doors unlocked, but I never used those words."

Erica checked her notes. "You said so the men would be 'taken care of'."

"Maybe I hoped they'd get a warning, be scared off, that kind of thing, but never once did I say anything about them being murdered."

"How did you think they'd be scared off?"

She shrugged. "I don't know. That part didn't have

anything to do with me. All I did was find these men on the app."

Erica cleared her throat. "Let's talk about the app. These men have been using it to find their next victims, but you work there. If you're so against men like Darren and Guy, how can you live with yourself, surviving on their money? Because that's how these apps make money —from the subscriptions men like Darren and Guy are paying for them."

"What better way to keep an eye on them than from within? I can see who they've been messaging, what they've been saying. I can see who their next victim is going to be and watch them get closer. How do you think I found Victoria Nestell and Neve? It was through their account details, being able to see these men had made contact with them." She gave a tiny smile. "Besides, not all people are like that. There are good romance stories on there, too. Maybe I've become a bit jaded, considering everything, but we do have real-life romances as well."

"You don't need to sell it to me," Erica said. "I've got no intention of ever joining one of those things."

Anna stared at her. "Well, never say never."

Erica wasn't about to get into that argument with her. "Who are the other women you've been working with?"

"No comment."

"Were you the one who pulled the trigger on Darren that night?"

"No, it wasn't me. I was elsewhere and I can give you my alibi. Same with Guy."

Erica suspected she'd planned for this. She'd made sure she had an alibi just in case everything blew up.

"Having an alibi doesn't make you innocent," she said. "Though of course we'll check it out. The question really is, Anna, if you didn't pull the trigger on the guns that killed Darren and Guy, who did?"

Anna stared Erica directly in the eye and said, "I have no idea."

"I don't believe you. Where is the gun that was used in the shooting?"

"How should I know? I've never even seen a gun in real life, never mind fired one."

Erica sighed and sat back.

They had two other women who would speak up against Anna in court, who would say they were manipulated into leaving their homes unlocked so she could send someone in to murder their partners. Victoria and Neve wouldn't walk away from this as free people, but the judge and jury would look at them more favourably if they testified against the ringleader.

Would they get a conspiracy to murder charge? It still meant a life sentence, even if Anna wasn't the one to shoot the gun.

The roots of this investigation ran deep, and she had no idea how many directions or branches they had.

FORTY

Erica had dropped Poppy off with Natasha first thing the following morning and then come in early to try and get a head start on the investigation. Though they had several people in custody, there was still a lot to do.

Her phone rang, a local number displayed on the screen.

She swiped to answer. "DI Swift," she said curtly.

The feminine voice on the other end sounded uncertain. "Oh, hello. Is this Poppy Swift's mum?"

Immediately, Erica shut off all other distractions from the office. She swivelled back around in her chair to face her desk and placed her fingertips to her temple.

"Yes, who's this?"

"It's Cindy calling from the school."

"Is everything okay?" Worry jarred through her.

"It's just that Poppy isn't in school today, but we haven't had an email or anything explaining her absence."

Erica's stomach dropped out of itself. "What? What do you mean she's not in school? She should be in school."

The woman cleared her throat down the line. "She hasn't been at form registration, and it doesn't look like anyone's seen her either. Did you not know that she wasn't at school?"

"No, I didn't, but my sister dropped her off this morning. Are her cousins in?"

Cindy hesitated. "Well, I haven't checked that yet, but they're not showing up on my list as absent."

Had Poppy been feeling sick that morning, so Natasha had kept her home? It was possible, but surely Tasha would have at least sent her a text to tell her, and Erica was sure she'd have let the school know. Natasha wasn't the type of person to forget to do something like that.

Erica tried to repress her growing panic. "Okay, let me contact my sister and find out if anything happened, and I'll get right back to you."

She took the woman's number and ended the call. Her hands were shaking. Where the fuck was Poppy? There had to be a reasonable explanation.

She called her sister, almost misdialling because her hands were shaking so badly.

Thankfully, Natasha answered right away. "Hi!"

Erica launched straight in. "Poppy's not at school. I've had them on the phone. Did you not drop her in this morning?"

Silence came down the line, then she said, "Of course I did."

"Shit. I was hoping you'd tell me that you'd kept her home. Would her cousins know where she is? She walked in with them, right?"

"Umm, I assume so, but they tend to spot their friends and then go off to walk in with them."

This was news to Erica. "So who does Poppy walk in with?"

"Honestly, she's normally on her own, but it's not as though I hang around to watch her or anything. I drop them all at the gates, so I assume they all get in okay."

"Well, they clearly don't, do they?" Erica said, close to tears.

"You could always have taken her yourself if you don't think I've been doing a good enough job," Natasha threw back at her.

This wasn't the time to argue, and, deep down, Erica knew her sister was right. She couldn't blame Natasha for this. Erica should have been paying more attention to her own child.

"Have you tried Poppy's phone?" Natasha suggested.

Erica felt like smacking herself in the forehead. And to think she was supposed to be the detective. "No, no, I haven't. I'm going to call her now."

"Phone me back and let me know if you get through to her. If you need me to get out on the streets and drive around, then I will. Can you think of any place she might have gone?"

"Only home."

Erica ended the call and then immediately swiped the screen for Poppy's number. She placed the phone back to her ear, but the call just went straight through to answerphone. Shit. She probably had it on 'do not disturb', or maybe she'd turned her phone off.

Or someone else has, a nasty voice suggested in her head.

Her breath caught. No, she didn't want to go down that path. Poppy was fine. She'd just bunked off school, that was all. Nothing terrible had happened to her. But in Erica's line of work, it was hard not to picture all the awful things that could happen to a young girl wandering London's streets. She could be hit by a car and left for dead in a ditch, or be grabbed by some weirdo and dragged behind some bushes. Maybe she'd been lured into the back of a van and was now being whisked away to another part of the country.

She shook her head and put her face in her hands. This wasn't helping anyone. She needed to be strategic about finding her, but right now all her brain was shouting at her was panic, panic, panic.

"Erica?"

She lifted her face from her hands at Shawn's voice, and at the sight of his concerned face, her eyes filled with tears.

"It's Poppy. She didn't go into school this morning, even though Natasha dropped her off. We don't know where she is, and she's not answering her phone."

"Shit. Did the two of you have a fight? Has she run away?"

"We're always fighting lately. She hates me."

"She does not hate you. She loves you. You're her safe space. She knows you'll always be there for her, no matter how she behaves, which is why it's safe for her to take her feelings out on you. I know it's not fair, but it means she loves you."

Erica sniffed. "It doesn't feel that way." Now wasn't the time to feel sorry for herself. "But it doesn't matter now. I just have to find her."

"We have to find her," he corrected. "Don't think for a second that I'm letting you do this by yourself."

He fixed her with his intense brown eyes, and she

knew he wouldn't take no for an answer. Besides, why the hell would she turn his offer down?

"Thanks, Shawn."

"She's like a daughter to me, too, Erica. That hasn't changed."

"I know. I'm sorry."

She was. Sorry for everything. Sorry for how life was so fucking shit sometimes that it didn't work out the way you wanted it to, even when you were decent people and tried to live your life right.

"Let's put a call out to all the uniformed police in the area," he said, "let them know a young girl is missing and that they need to be on the lookout. I assume she'd be wearing her school uniform."

"Honestly, I don't know. She might have changed out of it, but I guess she'd still definitely have her rucksack."

"Okay, and I've got a recent photograph I can circulate, too."

She was so grateful to have him take charge.

Her phone rang, snatching her attention. For a split second, she thought it was going to be Poppy, but then she saw Natasha's name onscreen.

"You didn't call me back," Tasha said when Erica answered.

"Sorry. She didn't answer. Shawn's helping me get the word out so we have uniformed police watching out for her. Can you phone the school for me and let them know to contact us if she happens to show up?"

"Yes, of course. I'll do it right away. God, Erica, do you think she's all right?"

"I really hope so. How did she seem this morning?"

"Quiet, but then she has been ever since..."

Erica knew what she was going to say. Ever since

Erica had lost the baby and Shawn had moved out. Poor Poppy had to deal with losing a chunk of her family all over again, and she'd started a new school at the same time. No wonder she was struggling. A wave of guilt washed over her. She wanted to tell herself this wasn't her fault, but was that true? The loss of the baby was something she'd struggled with as well. Had she put herself in harm's way? Had she somehow willed herself to lose the pregnancy because she'd never been one hundred percent sure that she'd wanted it? Each week that had gone by since the loss, she'd found herself counting how many weeks she'd have been pregnant by now, how close she'd have been to having a new child in her life, and it broke her heart. She should be thinking about maternity leave and nesting, and instead she was fearing the loss of the only child she had.

Erica shook herself out of it. Wallowing in her grief wasn't going to help Poppy now.

Shawn had gone back to his desk to make some calls. Should she phone round the hospitals, see if anyone matching Poppy's description had been brought in?

She prayed Poppy was just sitting in a park somewhere, ruminating on how much she hated her mother and her new school.

Word about Erica's missing daughter had quickly spread around the office. While they were all busy with the case, there was nothing more important than supporting a member of the team when they were needed, and everyone cared about both Erica and Poppy.

Within fifteen minutes, everyone was motivated to search for the missing girl. Local streets and parks would be searched. Access to CCTV and street cameras had been requested, so they could try to follow Poppy's route after she'd been dropped off at school.

She suddenly remembered that she had a tracking app on her phone. It was designed to find Poppy's phone if she lost it, but maybe it would work to find Poppy as well. She hadn't needed to use it before, and wasn't even completely sure how it worked, but she was sure someone in the office would.

"Does anyone know how to use the 'find my iPhone' app?" she called out across the office.

Lewis jumped to his feet. "Yeah, of course. Let me see." He held out his hand for her phone, and she handed it over. "I assume Poppy is on your account?"

"Yeah, she is. It's all in my name."

He nodded, his head bent over her phone as he worked it with both thumbs. It made her single finger swiping look old school.

"Her last known location, at least according to her phone, was here." He showed her the phone screen and pointed at a position on the map.

"Shit. That's miles away from school. What the hell is she doing there? She must have jumped on a bus or got the Tube or something."

Shawn joined them again, and she showed him the phone with its location.

Again, those negative thoughts tried to push their way into her head. "What if Poppy hasn't gone anywhere willingly and someone has forced her into a car?"

Shawn remained calm. "If that had happened, they wouldn't have let her keep her phone. The first thing a kidnapper would have done is take it off her and either toss it or destroy it."

She knew she was catastrophising, but couldn't seem to stop herself. "Maybe they didn't know she had it."

"Then she'd have used it to try and contact you in some way. Poppy's a smart kid."

She wished she could be as composed as he was.

"I need to get over there, see if she's still in that area."

"Of course. I'll drive."

Being the senior detective, Erica normally drove, but she was too shaky and panicky to drive safely. "Thank you."

"I'll feed back to the officers on the ground that we have a possible last known location," Lewis offered.

"Thank you, DC Crowe," she said gratefully.

They left the office and hurried out to the car.

Before she got in, she paused and spun back to face Shawn.

"Oh my God, what if something terrible has happened to her?" she blurted. "What if someone's taken her? You know the kind of people who exist in this world? We're not sheltered enough to believe this doesn't happen to people like us."

"Hey, hey, take a breath. She'll be okay. We'll find her."

Automatically, he reached for her, and she allowed herself to be pulled against his chest. He was so solid and familiar, and for a second, she felt like she was home. Her arms found their own way around his body, and he squeezed her tight.

"We'll find her," he said again. Then his hands were cupping her face, his fingers in her hair.

She tilted up her chin, and his mouth pressed to hers.

She kissed him back, wanting, needing this, more than she'd realised.

For the first time in months, she felt her world steady beneath her feet again. He was her rock, the person she leaned on. When something happened in her day, he was the person she wanted to call to tell about it. When she was upset, he was the one who calmed her. When she had something to celebrate, he was the one she wanted to pop the cork to the champagne.

He broke away. "Shit, I'm sorry. That was inappropriate."

"No, please, Shawn. Don't be sorry. I needed that."

She'd have carried on, if she'd had the time, would even have told him that maybe they should go back to the house now and see where this moment led, but her thoughts were on her missing daughter.

They were far from perfect. Their lives and history together was messy.

But wasn't that just life? How was it possible to spend years with the same person without there being some heartache thrown in?

He gathered up her hands in his much bigger ones, held them tight, and then brought them to his lips for another kiss.

"Let's go and find our girl."

She nodded, and he released her.

Erica went around to the passenger side and climbed in, and Shawn got behind the wheel.

"We need to head east," she said, checking the location on the phone.

"Got it."

As Shawn drove, Erica kept her phone gripped in her hand, constantly glancing at the screen, praying Poppy would call. She typed out a text message to her daughter.

<Please call and let me know you're safe. I'm not angry. Just worried. I love you.>

She did the same on WhatsApp, and then tried to call her again, but it still continued to go to an automatic answerphone.

He drove as fast as he dared without using the lights and siren. She gave him directions, taking them away from the city.

"You know where we're close to?" Shawn said finally.

"Where?"

"My aunt's place."

Erica stared at him. "Do you think she's gone to see her? I mean, we haven't been round there lately. I keep meaning to take her but...well, you know."

"It's awkward," he confirmed.

Despite her turmoil, she found the corners of her mouth lifting. "Yeah, it's super awkward."

"I should have taken her myself." Shawn shook his head. "I didn't think she might be missing them."

"She's been missing all of you," Erica said sadly. "I'd thought that my side of the family was enough, but it's not. She needs all of you, too."

He reached over and took her hand over the top of the handbrake. He squeezed her fingers. "It'll be all right."

He released her hand again, and she found herself wishing he hadn't. How could she say to him that she wished they could go back? It was impossible. Right now, she just needed to focus on finding Poppy. Had she really gone to see Shawn's aunt? She remembered all the fun family dinners they'd had around Gloria's cramped kitchen table. How Poppy had practically glowed at the older woman's attention. She'd never had a grandmother figure in her life, and the other woman had filled that gap.

Like losing the baby sibling, and the father figure in Shawn, she'd also lost Shawn's aunt.

"Fucking hell." She covered her face with her hands. "Poor Poppy. She's been having a difficult time at school as well. I think the transition has been harder than she'd expected. There's a lot of mean girl types at high school, and she's been feeling like she doesn't quite live up."

"That's rubbish. Poppy is the coolest kid I know."

Erica gave him the side-eye. "You're not a twelve-year-old girl."

"That obvious, huh?"

She thumped him on the thigh. "Stop it."

"Stop what?"

"Trying to make me laugh. Now is not a laughing time."

He took his eyes off the road to glance over at her. "I know, but that doesn't stop me wanting to see you smile."

Her heart clenched. "Shawn..."

"I know," he said. "You don't have to say it."

Say what? She wanted to say, that we're fucked? That this is never going to work? That it's not destined to be? She wanted to cry all over again.

"I didn't mean to mess everything up," she said instead.

"No. Me neither."

Shawn's phone buzzed. He glanced at the screen. "It's Gloria. Can you answer it?"

Erica didn't hesitate. "Gloria, it's Erica here. Do you have news on Poppy."

"Yes, she's with me at the house. I'm going to assume from the panic in your voice, and that it's the start of a school day, that she's not supposed to be here?"

"Oh, thank God." She mouthed 'she's there' at Shawn

who smiled and nodded in return. "We're on our way to you now. We're only about ten minutes away. We had an inkling that she might be heading to your place."

Gloria gave a chuckle. "Bad for her that she's got two detectives as parents." She caught herself. "Well, you know what I mean."

"Can you make sure she doesn't run off again?"

"She doesn't look like she's going anywhere. She's on the sofa with the cat, and I've given her a piece of my banana bread."

Erica blew out a breath. "Thanks, Gloria. I appreciate you taking care of her. We'll be with you shortly."

She ended the call and then swapped Shawn's phone for her own. She put a call out on the radio so the local uniformed police were aware, then started making the rounds to let everyone know that Poppy had been located and was safe. Natasha was first on her list, then she'd phone the school.

"Any news?" Tasha asked anxiously, picking up after only one ring.

"Yeah, we've got her. She's safe."

"Oh, thank goodness for that. I've been going out of my mind, blaming myself for not watching her go through the gates."

"It's not your fault. She's old enough that we should be able to trust her to walk into school by herself. I'm sorry I snapped earlier. I was just worried, and I took it out on you."

"It's okay, I get it. You trust me with Poppy, and I let you down."

"You didn't, Tasha. I promise. It's me who's let Poppy down by not being there for her enough. I'm going to put in for some holiday time just as soon as I get this case closed. God knows, I should have taken some ages ago. I'm surprised my boss hasn't strong-armed me into doing so by now."

"By the time the case is closed?" Natasha said, her tone sceptical.

"Yeah, yeah, I know. There's always another case, but I need to prioritise my family. I haven't been doing that enough lately."

She had no idea if taking a couple of weeks off so she could drive her daughter to school, and be there when she got home, so they could cook dinner together and talk about their day was going to be enough to fix things between them, but she had to try.

They arrived at Gloria's, and Shawn found a parking spot on the street outside. Gloria was already waiting in the open doorway, and she showed them into the house to where Poppy was still sitting in the lounge, any evidence of the banana bread long gone.

Erica rushed over to her.

"Poppy, thank God."

She pulled her daughter into a hug, burying her nose against the top of her soft head. It was only a couple of inches below her own now. She squeezed her tight. "Do you know how worried I've been? How worried we've all been? We've had police on the streets searching for you."

"Sorry, Mummy." It had been a while since she'd called her mummy instead of mum. "Do you think I'm going to get in trouble with school? I don't want to end up in detention."

"Don't worry about school, okay? I'll speak to them and explain that there's been a lot going on at home lately. I'm sure they've had to deal with kids doing a lot worse than not going in there."

Poppy spotted the other person in the room with them.

"Hi, Shawn." She seemed embarrassed. "I'm sorry I made everyone worry. I just didn't want to go in today."

"You could have told your aunt."

"I did, but she said I had to go in. It's the law."

"Well, she's right about that. But I'm sure the occasional day off never hurt anyone." He gave her a wink and then turned to Erica. "And that applies to you, too."

"Yeah, you're right."

"I can handle things at the office. Gibbs knows you've had a family emergency."

Erica didn't want to look as though she was rewarding her daughter for skipping school, but sometimes it was important not to play by the rules. Poppy running away to Gloria's had been a cry for help. Poppy had been trying to tell everyone how unhappy she'd been, but none of them had taken enough notice. It had required this dramatic event for her to get their attention.

"How about lunch and the cinema, and maybe a bit of shopping?" Erica offered.

Poppy's eyes went round. "Really?"

"Yes, but don't make a habit of it, okay? Next time, there will be a very different reaction."

Poppy gave a tiny smile. "There won't be a next time, I promise."

"Better not be," Erica said with a warning tone.

FORTY-ONE

Neve had been released pending investigation.

Now she was back in the house, except she wasn't sure if it even felt like her house anymore. How could someone who'd only been in her life for such a short time have created such a huge impact? Guy had wreaked havoc, and, even now he was dead, this still wasn't over.

The doorbell rang, and Neve cringed. She prayed it wouldn't be the media. They'd been crowded outside the police station when she'd been released, shouting questions at her. Half the news reports portrayed her as a cold-hearted killer, conspiring to murder her boyfriend, while the other half said she was a victim.

Neve wasn't even sure which version was true.

Still shaking from all the stress and sleep deprivation, she went to answer the door.

"Mum?"

Neve saw her daughter standing on the doorstep, and she burst into tears.

"Oh, Mum, I'm so sorry," Chloe cried. "Why didn't you call me?"

She opened her arms, and Neve fell into them.

"I didn't want you to see me like that, locked away like some criminal."

"I'd never think of you like that. Never."

"I was ashamed," Neve sobbed.

"I blame myself for encouraging you to date him," Chloe said, squeezing her tight. "I got all excited as well. I would never have done that if I'd known."

"I wouldn't have got excited either, if I'd had any idea what kind of man he was."

She untangled herself from her daughter's arms and hustled her inside the house, closing the door behind them. She swiped at the tears on her cheeks.

"He got his comeuppance, though," Chloe said, her eyes hard.

"Don't say that, Chloe. No one deserves to die."

Chloe arched an eyebrow and didn't reply.

Neve let out a sigh. "I don't know how I'm ever going to trust anyone again."

"Oh, Mum, you will. I know it won't be easy, but men like Guy are the abnormality here. Most people are decent."

"It should probably be the least of my worries, considering there's still a chance I could spend the rest of my life behind bars. My love life is hardly going to be much of a priority in prison."

"That's not going to happen. You didn't kill Guy."

"Not directly, no, but I played my part."

"I don't believe that," Chloe said harshly. "I know you. You're good and kind, and you've only ever wanted the best for people. You didn't know what they were going to do."

"I left the door unlocked."

Chloe threw up her hands. "Yeah, so they could come in and rob his wallet or something. The prosecution will have to prove that you knew without a shadow of a doubt that they were going to enter your home to murder him, and they can't prove that because it didn't happen."

Neve sniffed and nodded. Had she known, though? Deep down, in the moment where he'd stood on her doorstep and told her he loved her, and she'd experienced such intense, visceral rage, had she known that they were going to kill him?

She thought perhaps she did, but it was a thought she planned to keep to herself.

"Thanks, love. I don't know what I'd do without you."

Chloe gave her a smile of sympathy and then said, "You know I can move back in, if you're lonely."

She lived in a house share in Deptford with three other girls. The place was pretty run-down and basic, but it gave her some independence.

Neve shook her head. "I can't ask you to do that."

"You're not asking. I'm offering. Honestly, my rent is extortionate anyway, and the landlord is saying he's going to put it up again when our tenancy agreement runs out next month. Plus, we have mice, and he doesn't give a shit. One ran out of the fruit bowl the other day and right across the kitchen counter."

Neve found herself laughing at the scene her daughter had described.

"Okay, maybe just until the investigation is over."

Chloe smiled. "Deal."

Neve would be grateful for her daughter's company and support. She hadn't said so out loud, but the thought of being alone in the house, with both the pressure of the investigation hanging over her head and knowing that Guy had died in her hallway, was just too much.

"What would I do without you?" Neve said, giving her daughter another hug. "Who needs a man when I've got my girl?"

FORTY-TWO

Erica lightly knocked on the door of her boss's office.

DCI Gibbs called for her to enter, so she did, slipping inside, and closing the door behind her.

She was planning to request to take some holiday time. It had been a while, and now the case was wrapped up, she had a little breathing space. Poppy would still be attending school, but it meant Erica could drop her off and pick her up, and be there in the evenings to cook for her. It also meant they wouldn't have any fears about being woken in the middle of the night because a body had been found.

"Aah, Erica," Gibbs said, "Well done on that case."

"Thanks, sir, though it's going to be some time before we get everyone connected to it, if we ever do. Who knows how widely the syndicate has spread. We're still investigating past cases and if they could possibly be connected. This thing goes back years."

"Well, I won't be around to see it out. I'm counting down the weeks now."

She realised if she took holiday time now, she was

going to miss the final few weeks of working with him. Still, it couldn't be helped. Her daughter definitely came before her boss.

"I hope you enjoy your retirement, sir. I bet Pamela is looking forward to having you home more."

He chuckled. "Well, I'm not so sure about that."

Erica knew this wasn't true. His wife, Pamela, had been trying to get him to slow down for years now. She'd been, understandably, worried about his health, and didn't think the job was helping. Erica just hoped that Gibbs didn't lose his purpose for getting up in the morning by retiring. She'd seen it happen to too many good people. Spending your entire life in the police force was a bit like being institutionalised, much like someone being in prison. Once they were released from the constrains of their job, they didn't know what to do with themselves.

"Pam wants us to travel," he said. "She thinks we should buy a motorhome." He gave a mock shudder. "The thought of being stuck in a tin can together while we fight about directions honestly sounds like hell to me."

Erica found herself laughing at the mental image. "Maybe you should try renting one for a holiday first," she suggested, "before you make the more permanent leap of buying one."

He considered this. "Yes, that sounds like a sensible idea. I'll suggest that to her."

"You never know, you might catch the travelling bug," Erica said.

His expression told her that he thought such a thing happening was unlikely.

A knock came at Gibbs' door, and Erica glanced over her shoulder as DCI Gibbs called, "Come in."

The door opened, and a heavy-set woman in a white shirt and a grey trouser suit walked in. Her mousy-brown hair was cropped short, and her eyes seemed too close together.

Bypassing Erica completely, the woman approached Gibbs' desk. He got to his feet and shook her hand.

"DCI Fenn. I wondered when you'd come and introduce yourself to everyone."

Erica's ears pricked up. *DCI Fenn?*

Gibbs gestured in Erica's direction. "This is DI Erica Swift. Erica, this is DCI Anette Fenn. She'll be your new boss after I retire."

Erica sensed the woman's gaze sweep up and down her body, as though she was assessing her, then DCI Fenn stuck out her hand in Erica's direction.

Erica put her hand in the other woman's meaty palm, and the two of them shook, matching polite smiles on both their faces.

"Ah, yes. DI Swift. I've heard about you. You're the one who got her husband murdered, is that right?"

Erica dropped the woman's hand and jerked back. "I'm sorry?"

She shot a glance over to DCI Gibbs to see if he'd had a reaction to what the other woman had said, but he just appeared sympathetic.

Fenn spoke more slowly, as though Erica was a child. "I said that your husband was murdered. That's right, isn't it? I've got the right person? Though that's not really something you forget or get muddled up."

Erica gritted her teeth. "Yes, my husband was killed by a madman."

"I'm terribly sorry for your loss. What a tragic thing to have happened."

She did seem sincere, and Erica found herself wondering if she'd misheard the earlier jibe.

"Thank you," she said.

Fenn gave another smile that didn't seem to quite reach her too-closely set eyes. "Well, I'm looking forward to working with you."

Erica remembered thinking that the team had too much testosterone in it. Now she had a woman for a boss. How was this going to go down?

She hoped she wasn't going to regret what she'd wished for.

THE END

Loved what you've read? Don't miss out on book fifteen of the series, The Chess Master! Order now from Amazon!

Get a free book when you sign up to M K Farrar's newsletter

mkfarrar.com

Exclusive offer for Erica Swift readers! Get 25% off your order using the following code at MK Farrar's direct store: NEPHKVYNSX66

Get great deals on eBooks, audiobooks, and signed paperbacks direct from MK Farrar at

mkfarrarbooks.com

Two teenagers are snatched from the gritty streets of East London, but only one is being looked for...the one they didn't mean to take.

Don't miss out on book fifteen of this heart-racing, British detective series. Order now from Amazon!

ACKNOWLEDGMENTS

My lovely dad passed away a few years ago, and, in the years that followed, my still fabulous mum has dipped her toe into internet dating. Being the overprotective daughter I am, my mind went to all kinds of horrors that might happen.

I will admit that the 'he's after your money' one was the first fears came to me, no matter how much she tells me no one is parting her from her cash! Over the past couple of years, she's kept me entertained with some of her dating app horror stories, which is where the idea for this story came from.

So thank you, Mum! I hope you've enjoyed the book.

I always need to also thank my editor, Emmy Ellis, and all my proofreaders, Jessica Fraser, Jacqueline Beard, and Tammy Payne. It always amazes me how many of those little weeds that are typos sneak their way into the book. I swear they're like whack-a-moles—I get rid of one and up pops another.

You all help to make my books so much better.

And finally, thanks to you the reader, for continuing to support me in this incredible journey that is writing.

Until next time!

MK Farrar

ABOUT THE AUTHOR

M K Farrar has penned more than thirty novels of psychological noir and crime fiction. A British author, she lives in the countryside with her three children and a menagerie of rescue pets.

When she's not writing—which isn't often—she balances out all the murder with baking and binge-watching shows on Netflix.

You can find out more about M K and grab a free book via her website, https://mkfarrar.com

She can also be emailed at mk@mkfarrar.com. She loves to hear from readers!

ALSO BY THE AUTHOR

LAW OF SANDTOWN

The Scorched Girls
Under the Surface
One Final Shot

Detective Ryan Chase Thriller

Kill Chase
Chase Down
Paper Chase
Chase the Dead
Silent Chase

CRIME AFTER CRIME

Watching Over Me
Down to Sleep
If I Should Die

Standalone Psychological Thrillers

Some They Lie
On His Grave
21 Days
In The Woods

Printed in Great Britain
by Amazon

51884159R00162